In Love with the Devil

A True Love Story
Written by: Raynelle Rumph

Hear no Evil
See no Evil
Love no Evil

For we wrestle not against flesh and blood, but against principalities, against powers, against the rulers of the darkness of this world, against spiritual wickedness in high places.

Ephesians 6:12 kjv

I dedicate this book to all of my readers. Every word was written with you in mind.

Table of Contents

Full Disclaimer

Nigga, you know who the fuck you are. Won't shit be changed to protect your privacy or feelings because you didn't change shit to protect mine. You wanted to be famous, how about I make you a fucking legend. Now clock that tea.

Trigger Warning:

To my readers, because I actually care about your mental health and wellness when reading my work. I must warn you that this book isn't for the soft at heart or sensitive. It depicts real life situations of mental, emotional and some physical abuse.

It discusses situations of gas lighting and delves into the heart of being under the control of a complete maniacal narcissist. For those who can relate to this type of domestic abuse and you still want to proceed, know that I'm right here with you and we can get through this together.

That being said from this point forward I will be talking to you directly as I would a friend, because I consider you (my reader) somewhat of a friend. Hell, I might as well call you friend, I'm about to divulge all my fucking business to your ass. But that's okay, it feels good to get this shit out to the world.

Since I'm calling you my friend, just know I will be talking to you as such. So, if you're one of them sensitive ass bitches that you can't say shit to, or someone who gets easily offended, this might not be the read for you; because bitch, this is how I talk. I don't mean any harm by it; I'm just being me.

So just know there will be a gratuitous use of profanity; like the words Fuck, Bitch, hoe, and nigga. You might even see combinations like Bitch nigga, Hoe ass nigga and my personal favorite Bitch fuck that hoe ass nigga. Don't be alarmed.
Some profanity may even be directed towards you. Please don't take offense, a little friendly fire ain't never hurt nobody. I'm just expressing myself; that's all. Telling this story is hard for me, this shit ain't easy, but it's necessary. With that being said, you've been warned.

The Devil is in the details

Introduction

*Alright, listen up bitch; I'm about to tell you
the deepest, most intimate details of my life
that I've never told anyone.
My thoughts, my fears, my
inadequacies. Bitch I'm going to lay it all
out on the line for you.
And you know what I don't want? I don't
want you sitting around this motherfucker
judging me; ok, that's what I don't need.
I don't need to hear about what I should've
done or what you would've done because
well bitch, it wasn't you; It was me.
All you need to do is fucking listen.
From this point forward, this will be a
judgement free zone.
I'm pretty sure in some aspect, your in-
denial ass can relate to the story I'm about*

*to tell you, but you'll never admit the shit;
and if you can't relate. Then I know for a
fact, you know someone that can. So just
shut the fuck up, sit back, and listen.
That's right, I said it. I don't give a fuck
about you buying no book either bitch. This
is how we're going to talk. Girlfriend to
girlfriend, Woman to woman. Real bitch to
real bitch. You feel me?
So find a comfortable spot to read in and
grab whatever calms your nerves. Your
glass of wine, cup of tea, coffee, blunts,
joints, or hookahs; bitch just relax is all I'm
saying because the contents of this book is
going to work up your nerves.
It might bring on flashbacks of Ray-Ray's
bitch ass and how he did you, it's okay
friend. Take a sip of wine and keep calm
we're going to get through this.
Put the children to bed because we don't
need you yelling at them. It's about to get
deep, and just like your baby daddy did;
bitch I'm about to give it to you raw.
Hell, you might get mad and feel like
reaching out and slapping your nigga. I*

don't advise you do that friend especially if you got the kind that'll hit your ass back........ We don't want no trouble. Just keep calm, grab your shit, I'm about to grab my wine and meet you on the next page. Okay, what're you waiting for, let's go!

Speak of the Devil
Chapter One

We've all heard the saying "Speak of the devil and he shall appear." Well, I didn't speak of anyone that night let alone the devil, but that didn't stop the motherfucker from appearing.

The sky was as dark as sin that night and the moon full and bright. That in itself should've been my first red flag. Everybody knows a full moon brings out the worst shit. If Michael Jackson's Thriller taught us anything it taught us that.

But I've never been one to heed the warning signs in life. I tend to stumble blindly into shit. I don't find out how deep the water is until I dive in, and by then it's too late; its either sink or swim.

That's just what I did when I met him. I dove head first into a cold, deep, pool of his bullshit. I remember the first time I laid eyes on the devil like it was yesterday. It was an unseasonably hot September night. I should've known evil was lurking nearby. Myself and my boyfriend at the time had just pulled up to a liquor store in the new neighborhood I'd just moved into.

Before you say anything, I already know what you're thinking. *Who meets someone at a liquor store?* Shit; *me.* What's the fucking difference between a bar, a night club and a liquor store? I'll wait. Hell; they all sell alcohol.

Anyway so, I got out and went in the liquor store leaving my boyfriend in the car. Once inside I noticed there were a group of guys in there already but I didn't pay them any attention; like I said, I was with my boyfriend.

Out of the four or five guys that were in there, two of whom I would later come to know as his brother and friend; he was the one to approach me.

"Damn, baby you got some big ass titties." That was the first thing he said to me, I swear.

Now, I know what you're thinking. *Why would you talk to him after that?* Well, the reason I didn't get an attitude with him, or ignore him like I normally would have; is because I was actually mad at my boyfriend.

We were tethering at the end of a shaky, seven-year relationship; that neither one of us wanted to let go of. Even though things were going as badly as they could go. I remember he and I were actually in the middle of a very big fight that night.

Asking him to come in the store and defend my honor against a group of guys didn't seem likely. Plus, he was outnumbered. I was only going to get his ass kicked anyway. So, it was best I handled the shit on my own.

Now when he made his comment about my titties, I'll admit it was a little out of pocket; but I didn't get mad or tell him off or anything. Shit, he wasn't lying. I do have some big titties. This was way before the BBL epidemic so I was still relevant.

Instead of making a scene, I sort of laughed it off. One of my many defense mechanisms.

However, when I looked up at him; I was pleasantly surprised. The little nigga was actually cute. He wasn't tall, dark, and handsome or no shit like that; but he was attractive. At least he was to me anyway.

"Hey beautiful, where's your man at?"

"In the car." I looked out the window gesturing to where my boyfriend was. He turned his head to follow my gaze, then turned back to me. "I don't give a fuck about that nigga. I'm trying to holler at you. You sexy as hell. I like what I see. Fuck wit me."

"Thank you, but I can't my boyfriend's in the car."

"Man, fuck that nigga. Let me get your number?"

We both know at some point I gave the nigga my number, because I wouldn't be telling this story if I didn't. Now, before you say anything, I already know what you're thinking. *How can you talk about him when you were in the wrong, for giving out your number; when you knew you already had a boyfriend.*

Try and keep up bitch. You're going to have to read between the lines on some shit. I can't explain every single detail to your ass.

Like I said, shit wasn't going well with my current relationship. We were damn near over; but still holding on for some reason. He wasn't shit either, by the way. Liar, cheater, drug addict, zero ambition. Need I go on?

To top it off. I had been consistently loyal to him before that night. What changed, I don't know. Maybe that full moon had brought out a change in everyone; or maybe the right temptation hadn't come along. For whatever reason, as discreetly as I could under my boyfriend's microscopic stare; I gave the Devil my number.

Once my purchase was completed, I made my way outside to where my boyfriend was waiting. I didn't say anything about the encounter for obvious reasons.

I got in the car, started it up, and began to pull off. He eyed me suspiciously as I pulled away from the liquor store. Being the lying, cheater that he was. It made him accuse me of doing the things that he did; even though I wasn't doing them.

But that night was different. I actually did the thing he was accusing me of.

"What, them niggas must've been trying to holler at you or something?" He asked, wondering if I would do the same things to him that he did to me. Deep down he knew he deserved that shit; but I never did it. The lack of evidence against me did nothing to ease his conscious. His tone was still accusatory, and was further pissing me off with him.

I wondered if he felt that way, why the fuck didn't he just get his ass out the car; and get his straightening? We both knew the answer to that question. Five against one, equals a fraction off that nigga's health. He didn't want to check them niggas; just me.

To be honest with you. I can't remember if I answered yes or no to his question. If I answered yes, it would've probably been to make him feel some type of way. If I said no, it would've probably been because; I didn't want to hear his fucking mouth.

Either way, his time was coming to an end. He could feel it. I have no remorse for it; because up until that night I had been nothing but faithful to his ass. You know how the nigga showed me his appreciation? By being the worst man, I'd ever met (up until that night). I was just counting the days until I could be free from him and all his bullshit.

What I didn't count on though, what neither of us knew at the time was that someone far more sinister than him was coming. The Devil's reign was about to begin and he was going to turn me every which way but loose.

You ever hear the saying out of the frying pan and into the fire?

Like I said before, I dove head first and bitch; it was sink or swim. Now before you go saying judgmental ass shit like: *That's what your ass gets, you should've stayed with the first one.* That nigga was no better. He was a habitual abuser of drugs and the relationship was toxic as fuck. He was a bad choice, I admit that. But again, I was young, I was twenty years old. I didn't know any better. As bad as that nigga was, he had nothing on the nigga to come.

I'm telling you this nigga; was evil, in its purest form. Where did he hide the horns? Up his ass, I'm guessing.

When I left the store that night, I had no intentions at all; let alone ill ones. It's not like I had made plans to meet up with the guy or anything. I was just going to keep him tucked away in my contacts, for safe keeping, when or if my relationship, came crashing down; and eventually it would.

Better the Devil you know

Chapter Two

Are you familiar with the saying, "Better the devil you know than the devil you don't" It's used to say it is better to deal with a difficult person or situation whom you are accustomed to dealing with rather than a new person or situation that could be much worse.

I wish someone had explained the depth of the meaning of that saying to me, before I made my choice. Not my choice to leave my previous boyfriend because I don't regret that at all, I had to do that. I do regret however the nigga I ended up with after him.

Ultimately, the relationship I was in came to a painful but necessary end. I abandoned the sinking ship and would've been much better for it, had I not climbed aboard the first shiny new vessel that promised to rescue me. But when you are alone for the first time in your life, in uncertain dark waters, the first thing you look for is someone to rescue you. You cling to them because in your mind they're saving you right? Wrong.

At first, I thought he was an angel, I thought this man must be heaven sent. I hadn't the slightest clue what I'd gotten myself into. But wait let me back it up a little bit, I'm getting ahead of myself.

Right before the end of my previous relationship, I started seeing him. Yes, this nigga has a name and no; I'm not going to say it. He doesn't deserve that type of notoriety from me. From here on out, I'm going to refer to his bitch ass as "The Devil" and you should too.

So, this demon, this demonic entity assigned from the pits of hell to destroy my life; called my phone a few days after I gave him my number. However, it wouldn't be until a few weeks later when we would actually hook up.

I was feeling alone in my current relationship and felt I could use a distraction to take my mind off of what I was going through. A cool new breeze to lift my spirits was just what I needed.

Howbeit, this nigga was walking pneumonia disguised as a breath of fresh air. At the time I was living in my brother's house with him, his girlfriend and four children. I was home alone one night when The Devil came knocking. He called, and asked if I wanted to meet up with him.

Feeling vindicated from the neglect and what I discovered my current man was doing behind my back. I took him up on the offer.

So, we met up, just to chill and hang out. You know get to know one another. I found out he was an aspiring artist. A rapper which should've been red flag number three, but again before you judge me keep in mind that I was young; I didn't know any better.

Although I didn't, I saw that he smoked weed; which was a far cry from the heavy drugs my current boyfriend was into so I didn't trip. I was privy to having a few drinks myself.

We each ended up doing our own thing but the vibe was still there. Meeting up for the first time on a non-date isn't something I'd do now, but hey, like I said; I was in my twenties. I didn't know any better, I was going through my shit in my relationship so the bar wasn't set too high at the time.

I was cool with just kicking shit for the moment, having someone to talk to that was actually listening to me. Over the past few weeks we'd talked exclusively over the phone and that was only when my boyfriend wasn't around.

So, the night we met up the chemistry was just as good as it was over the phone. He was still very attractive to me, as he was the first night I saw him in the liquor store. Another thing that made the connection stronger, was that bravado demeanor he possessed at the liquor store was gone.

He was humbler, nicer and respectful even. I could only conclude that the first encounter wasn't the real him, that he was only acting that way in front of his friends, which should've been red flag number four but who the fuck pays attention to red flags anyway?

The prissy, lady in me, wants me to tell you that we had a lovely evening talking and at the end of the night he drove back to his home and I went back to mine.

But the real bitch that lives deep down inside of me with her, is forcing me to tell you the truth. You don't understand; I must oblige; this heifer is loud and ghetto. She forces me to say things, phony motherfuckers would never admit to. All in the name of keeping it real or better yet, how she puts it; keeping it a hundred or keeping it a buck.

She just won't let me be great in front of people.

So in the vein of keeping it a hunnit, I did go home; but if you're thinking I went alone that wasn't the case.

Now when I started this book, I didn't promise you a glamorous fairytale love story. You know what the fuck you signed up for. I promised you the truth and that's what the fuck you're about to get.

Also, when you and I started this conversation; it was to my understanding that this was a judgement free zone?

If I'm wrong let me know; because one thing, I don't like is a fake phony hoe that act like she ain't never did shit. Sitting there with your lip tooted all up at me and bitch you probably done laid more niggas to rest than the Chicago city morgue.

But that's neither here nor there, I'm not going to talk about you like that because you're my friend remember, we besties now, you bought my book.

Anyway, best friend so sexual activities took place that night but we didn't have intercourse. Don't worry friend, prophylactics were used as I believe in safe sex. Shit, it is what it is; I have no regrets, well actually, I may have one.

I wish I'd taken him up on his offer to eat my pussy that first night because I would've known how whack that shit was before I fell in love with his ass and we wouldn't be having this conversation.

But I didn't have any saran wrap, which didn't really matter to this nigga because he was still willing to do the shit. Red flag number five. *Are you keeping count?*

I know what you're thinking; *why didn't y'all have sex if y'all was doing all that?* Damn, you a nosy bitch. Its ok girl go on; get all the tea.

Well, I still had my current boyfriend on my mind and even though he wasn't shit, I was still battling with the morale of it all. I know it doesn't sound like it, but I really was a good girl. I've only been in three serious relationships in my entire life and I was faithful in every last one of them, if that ain't a good girl I don't know what the fuck is.

The first relationship I was in was with my boyfriend I had in my teens, the second was the one I was with in my early twenties you know, the drug addict; and then there was this nigga, The Devil.

I know it doesn't make sense to you, so I'm not even going to try to explain it. All I know is that it made sense to me at the time. I guess I was just programmed that way.

Look, I'm not about to argue with you over some shit that happened over ten years ago, it's done; it's over. All I can tell you is that the shit happened; bitch, get over it.

So, we saw each other a few more times after that night, he would mainly drive to my house to visit me. We'd chill watch movies grab something to eat all the while my MIA boyfriend was nowhere to be found. He was off doing him, coming around whenever he felt like it.

So, eventually I figured what the hell, I might as well give him some; because shit, why not? The first time we had sex, I must say I was unimpressed.

It was like I had been fucked by a jack rabbit. Now I already know what you're thinking. *Damn bitch if it was like that, why did you stick around so long?* Bitch, I just did, okay. You and these fucking questions hoe.

For me it wasn't about the sex. He came in and was doing things that I didn't even notice I wasn't getting from my boyfriend anymore. It was just the attention, the companionship the interest he showed that seemed genuine at the time.

So what if he didn't drop the dick down on me like I was used to getting. I'd been getting that for the last seven years and all that shit brought with it was headache, pain and tears.

I wanted something different, something real, something concrete. Sex wasn't the end all be all. Hell, really sex is what you make it when you find someone you really care about.

Eventually, my body adjusted to the drastic change in sexual altitude. I was flying on a much lower level, but shit, I was still flying.

I had enough skills for the both of us anyway. So, I took my jack rabbit under my wings and molded him like clay until he fit me just right; literally.

You're probably sitting there thinking, *damn bitch you must be bitter; look how you're talking about this man.* First off this is not a man, this is The Devil and as long as you think he is a man the more you're going to empathize with him and think dumb shit like that.

How are you going to be my friend and be on his side at the same time, like come on now; which side are you working?

Secondly If you're worried about this motherfucker's feelings, don't be. That nigga ain't got none, trust me; I know. Didn't I say he was The Devil.

Third of all and most importantly if I don't tell the truth, I might as well not tell the story at all. There's one thing everyone that knows me know about me, especially him and that is that I don't lie.

So, fuck what it looks like fuck what it sounds like, it is what it is. Why are you sitting there looking sideways for, I don't know. I'm only speaking the truth, not my truth, not his truth. There's only *one* truth.

So, this budding, blossoming new romance was growing on me. Slowly but definitively, so much so that my current relationship had lost its appeal and I was finally able to dish my old boyfriend out a taste of his own medicine.

That didn't go over as well as I thought it would. No matter how much dirt a motherfucker does to you, try to turn that shit back around on him and he'll fight you tooth and nail.

For a nigga that did everything imaginable to ruin the relationship. When it was finally over, he just couldn't take it, this motherfucker refused to leave without a fight.

Hell Bent and Hell Bound
Chapter Three

I had no clue I was going from bad to worse. At the time I thought I was making the right move for myself, with the right person. I was leaving this awful, dead-end relationship behind and putting myself in a position to gain some momentum and finally move forward in life.

After seven years of oppression, dealing with drug addiction, cheating and lies, I was done being stagnant. I was through; fed up. I was ready for something new, ready for the life I dreamed about. The love I deserved and I was hell bent on making it happen whatever the cost. Little did I know, the train I'd boarded was bound for hell. I was on a downward descent into darkness and didn't even know it.

In the beginning I'm not going to lie, it was beautiful. We spent so much time together. I mean we did everything together and went everywhere together side by side. We talked to each other every day about any and everything. Private and public displays of affection were plentiful.

One of the things that attracted me the most to him was the fact that we shared a lot of the same interests. He was heavily into the bible and the lord, which was impressive to me because I hadn't met a man that was so young and grounded in their faith like he was. I thought I had a man I could look up to that could lead me on the right path and help me stay grounded and focused; someone that I could grow with spiritually.

In the beginning we would pray, read the bible and even go to church together. I know you're asking yourself,

So, how did he go from deacon to devil? Just hold on I'm about to get there.

Right out of the gate, the devil and I made a lot of plans concerning our future together. Everything I wanted in life he wanted. His optimism was magnetic; it was one of the qualities that drew me to him. He believed that we could do anything. I never tapped into that type of outlook on life until I met him.

Being with him was such a refreshing and welcoming change. At first, I couldn't find a flaw in him or our relationship. That's because I didn't know that at the time, our relationship was built on a foundation of deceit.

He'd carefully laid each lie brick by brick. Our home, so beautiful looking from the outside, was nothing more than a house of lies. So carefully decorated with deception to the point that I couldn't find my way out even if I tried.

Immediately following the breakup with my previous boyfriend, I moved out of my brother's house and across town into my own apartment where the devil eventually followed, visiting me quite often. It wasn't long before his one or two-night sleep overs turned into week long stints until he ultimately moved himself into my newly acquired space.

Prior to us living together he would always visit me at my brother's house so I really didn't have much knowledge of his living arrangements or his financial status for that matter.

What he told me was that he lived with his friend, his friend's girlfriend and her children. Another red flag that went unheeded. It wasn't until sometime after he moved in with me that I learned he was actually living with a girl or should I say his girlfriend because he never even until this day admitted that he was in a relationship with that girl.

I would soon come to learn that the girl he was living with which was a white girl, her mother and her children were best friends with another white girl he was in a relationship with prior to entering into a relationship with her. A hot mess child.

I learned from him that she was a meth addict. Normally all of this would've sent me running for the hills. But I'd just gotten out of a relationship with a person that suffered from addiction (to a different drug) so, I could understand wanting to get away from something like that.

I mean after you've offered all the help you can offer; at some point you have to save yourself; if they refuse to get help. So instead of this driving a wedge between us, it actually brought us somewhat closer together.

The part about him ending up with her best friend, red flag number.... well, you get it by now. Anyways, under normal circumstances I would've never entered into a relationship with someone like that, but given the situation and the fact that in other areas he was killing it; in terms of how he made me feel and the connection we were making. Who cared about the mistakes he made before me?

We were together now and we had the potential to make it. I did feel bad after learning that the car he used to drive to my brother's house and visit me in, belonged to the white girl he was with at the time he was seeing me. I don't play that shit, I'm not one to break up happy homes, but he swore they weren't together.

I didn't believe him but I did believe that they were over and he wanted to be with me exclusively, so I didn't let how we got together interfere with us being together. Besides, I couldn't be too judgmental, given the fact that I too entered the relationship fresh out of one.

The saying goes, how you get them is how you lose them. I figured that wouldn't apply to me because I had no knowledge of this relationship; like he had of mine, until he and I were in one of our own.

How I first found out about the girl, was one day we were at my apartment and she called him stranded on the side of the road with her children in her car and she was asking for his help.

We were in the dining room for some reason that day, I can't remember what we were doing specifically; I just know that's where we were, when his phone kept ringing repeatedly.

I mean the text were coming in back-to-back and he was ignoring them. I'd seen this type of behavior before, with the last nigga; so I wasn't going to ignore the shit the second time around. I was going to set a precedent, nip this shit in the bud. So, I asked him;

"Who keeps calling your phone like that?"

"Nobody."

"What do you mean, nobody? How can nobody blow your phone up like that?" I was starting to get agitated because this shit was starting to feel all too familiar.

"That's just this girl."

"What girl?" He had my full attention now because I really wanted to know what girl this nigga was talking about. He had been at my apartment for the last few weeks. When we got together, I was under the impression that he was single, because that's what the fuck he said. I hadn't heard anything about a girl before so why am I hearing about one now?

"That's this girl I was talking to before I met you." He said nonchalantly like the shit meant nothing. I guess in a way it didn't because if she was before me then it really didn't matter. It's just that he knew about my situation and the nigga before him, so why did he keep his shit quiet?

I could think of no other reason than he was with the girl the whole time I was with my ex, and if that's true, then why not be open and honest about his shit like I was about mine? Why say you were living with your friend and his girlfriend?

I truly believe he did it to paint this narrative about him like he was this single good guy, that was just misunderstood and had some bad breaks in life. I bought right into that shit. Now here he was telling me about this white girl who I knew nothing of, that had been in the mix all along.

"Well, why is she calling you now?"

"Her car broke down and she's stranded on the side of the road with her children." He said showing me the texts. After reading them and seeing pictures of her and her children, I kind of felt bad for the girl. In the texts she was wondering where he's been and why he wasn't responding to her or coming to help her and her children. She literally said she had no one else to call for help.

"Are you going to help her?"

"Nope."

"Why not?" I was genuinely curious, I mean there were pictures of her and her children in his phone. I can't remember if they were in his phone, in the text, or just on social media but I saw them.

The children weren't his or anything, they were white but if he had been playing step daddy, why didn't he have a moral sense to at least help them get off the side of the road?

In the pictures I saw the car he was driving to my house and put two and two together that he was driving her car to come see me at night. I had ridden in this poor girl's car. I should've known right then the type of person I was dealing with.

Now, here she was in a tough spot in her car; that this nigga probably ran into the ground and he was ignoring her cries for help.

He didn't have a car of his own, and I wasn't about to lend him mine to help his ex, but if it had been me, I would have tried to send some long-distance help, a tow truck or something but that's just me.

In short, he left her and her children stranded but that wasn't the last we'd hear of Becky, she and her mother gave him some legal woes. Took his ass to court, he was arrested and everything for some shit he'd done to them while they were together.

Of course I had to bail him out. What's crazy is he talked so much shit about her and her mother stealing from him. He said his clothes and jewelry would always come up missing.

I'm like you mean that little duffel bag you got in my closet? Nigga, ain't no jewelry in there. Ain't shit in there but three outfits and a half at the most. I figured he was probably saying that to justify having so little.

In court though, I found out that the whole time; he was the one conning them.

If only I'd known then, that the same things he did to her; he was going to do to me. Here you go. *Of course, he's going to do the same shit he did to her to you, girl; what made you think you were so special?* Bitch, he did. Obviously.

He made it seem like she was this terrible person. That her and her mother were using him; taking him for everything that he had. I would soon find out, that the nigga ain't have shit for nobody to take. Not a pot to piss in or a window to throw it out of, as my dear mother would say.

Before we started living together it was easy for him to pretend to be more than he actually was. I found out the hard way that this man had nothing to his name; not one thing.

The car he drove belonged to his ex-girlfriend. All he brought with him was one duffel bag with a few articles of clothing; barely a week's worth.

You have to understand that, prior to us moving in together we didn't see one another every day but now we were seeing each other on a daily basis. I could see that the person he claimed to be, was far from the person he was.

He lived in a fantasy world in his own head, claiming to be this big hustler but having nothing to show for these outlandish, outrageous, claims to fame. He was nothing more than a two-bit hustler and a pathological liar. How could he be anything else; I mean, The Devil has always been known as the father of lies.

Which was quite fitting for him, because everything that came out of his mouth was a fucking lie.

In the beginning I believed him, not because I was gullible but because I was hopeful and I believed in him. I thought he possessed the potential, to be the man he claimed to be.

So, I didn't call him out for not exhibiting those qualities right off the bat, I figured if I nurtured our relationship, supported him and stood behind him one hundred percent; he would get there eventually, right? Wrong.

I was so fucking wrong, and the problem with being that fucking wrong, is the heavy price you pay, for gambling so big. They say life is one big gamble. Well, if that's true; then I was about to lay all my cards on the table. The Devil was the one for me and I was willing to bet my life on it. In many ways I did.

I was all in, before the turn or the flop. All I needed was a king, to complete my full house. What I got in the end, was royally fucked instead.

I'd managed to pull another jackass.

The Devil Wears New Balance?
Chapter four

They say the devil wears many disguises. I never thought he would come walking into my life in a pair of size thirteen new balances though. Now before your coochie go to getting all wet. They weren't his shoes or his size, so calm down. Bitch I know, he fooled me too okay.

The thing with the new balances, and I have nothing against new balance shoes or the men that wear them by the way; but I was not accustomed to men that wore that brand of shoes. Again, nothing wrong with it, just new territory for me that's all.

Not to mention the fact that it would've been less noticeable if the shoes actually belonged to him. Now this memory burned a hole into my brain, so much so that it found its way into my book and for good reason too. Just hold on I'm about to get to the point.

Now, did I ever see him personally wearing the shoes? Honestly, I can't remember if I did or if I didn't.

All I know is that when I was cleaning my apartment one day, I came across them in the closet. The sheer length of the shoe was abnormally larger than what I knew his feet to be. So, when he came home from out in the streets, not working mind you. Just out and about, going to and fro; seeking whom he can devour. You know, doing devil shit.

I asked him where did the shoes come from? He told me that they were his friend's shoes. That he let him wear them or have them or whatever the case may be; I can't remember.

All I know is that somehow, the shoes ended up in the nigga's duffel bag. So, he had to have put them in there. He made a choice, a conscious decision, to pack a pair of size thirteen new balance shoes; that didn't belong to him and bring them to my house, with the intention of wearing them.

That, along with the scarcity in contents of the duffel bag was my first, real indication that this nigga was in dire financial straits.

Now, I wasn't a rich bitch by far, but I could take care of myself. I had a car, my own apartment; and of course my own clothes and shoes. I worked at a salon during that time and I didn't have to ask anyone for shit.

So, you can imagine the alarm bells that were going off in my mind, when he moved himself in with me; and it dawned on me, that he had no means to contribute to the household finances.

Now, I'm a resourceful motherfucker. I don't give up easily. You hand me a problem and I will solve that shit, no matter how long it takes me to get it done; trust, it will get done.

Most women would have called him a lost cause. Well, not most; a few if we're just being honest but we know you bitches will never do that; so we're going to pretend like it's just me.

Anyway, the problem solver in me didn't see a lost cause, it saw a simple problem that needed a simple solution. If only it were at all that simple.

Let me ask you a question friend, if you have a perfectly good outfit to wear out, but there's just one tiny flaw in it; you don't get rid of the whole outfit, do you?

Hell no, you fix that shit up, make it look good, because you know it looks and feels good on you. Sometimes you have to make that shit work, and that's exactly what I planned to do with his ass. I was going to make that nigga work.

So, I took him job hunting, needless to say, the devil had another plan.

What I wish someone had told me, was that an adult male, with no job, was not just a tiny flaw in your outfit but a major wardrobe malfunction; that could have you ass out, if not handled properly.

Believe you me, this nigga came up with all kind of excuses as to why he wasn't able to find a job, main one being that he was a convicted felon. Hell of a way to find out when you take your man job hunting but I wanted to be as optimistic as possible.

Another sign I ignored, that would've let me known hazardous conditions were up ahead; was around the time I first met him. During the time I lived with my brother. One night, the nigga called me and asked if I had ten dollars he could borrow. I don't even know why he used the term borrow, that would imply that he had the intention to pay it back; when, if you don't know by now, he didn't.

I remember that night well, because I'd been arguing with my boyfriend and was in a mood when he called me. I didn't want to answer but I did; and child what for, because when the nigga asked me could he "borrow" ten dollars; I went up on his ass. As I should have.

Afterwards, he tried to bow out of the conversation as gracefully as he could. After I hung up, I don't know why but my soft-hearted ass felt bad for chewing him out. I was like he's been cool up until this point and what's ten dollars? Maybe he needed the shit and here I go being a complete bitch about it because I'm mad at someone else.

So, the next conversation that night, whether it was me who called him or whether he called me back. I offered to give him the ten dollars; which he graciously accepted. He stopped by and picked up the money later that night. I remember thinking, what was so important, he had to ask me; of all people? We didn't have that type of relationship; and why ten dollars? There was nothing significant, you could get with ten dollars. I figured it was as useless to him, as it was to me

I could have gotten out right then and there, and I should've. I mean I was only in up to my ankles. I really didn't have any skin in the game yet. I could have pulled out if I wanted to, but I didn't want to. There were some good qualities there, I just had to bring them out.

I figured what harm could it do to help him get back up on his feet; hopefully not those size thirteen new balances though but up into something better.

I had no idea that better, was him squeezing his size ten feet, into my size eight and a half air force ones. He had to go down a whole size and a half to fit them.

I couldn't decide which was worse. The size thirteen new balances or watching your man parade around the neighborhood in your shoes, pretending like they were his. I eventually let him have them, much like I did everything else. I mean what else could I do? I felt sorry for the nigga.

Sympathy for the Devil
Chapter Five

Anyone that knows me, knows the first thing about me is that I'm a good person. Yes, despite what you may feel, from this short conversation of ours; it's true. I'm not making the shit up and it's not a matter of opinion either; it's a known fact.

I have a heart of gold; I'm always trying to help people. I don't know why; I'm just programmed that way, I guess. Strangers on the street, someone in need of help; I sometimes go out of my way for another person's benefit; sometimes.

Not trying to toot my own horn or anything, it's just the way I am. Now, if I'm like that with strangers; how do you think I am with family, friends, or significant others? A true treasure is all I'm going to say. It's a blessing to come into contact with me and especially to be loved by me.

People tell me all the time that I'm "a good person" that I have "a good heart". When I was younger, I thought it was a compliment, but as I got older and dealt with more people; I found that people with bad hearts, tend to prey on the ones with good ones.

It's gotten to the point, where I hate to hear people call me a good person. How I translate that now is, "You a stupid mother fucker, how can I fuck you over?" It's sad too because I love helping people. I learned the hard way though, that you can't help everybody.

Not everyone wants your help, they just want to help themselves to whatever you have that they can use. The devil was no exception. I thought I was doing this nigga a favor when I looked out for him until he got back on his feet.

I thought that my kindness would be repaid with appreciation, love and gratitude. The love wasn't a requirement, however it would've been nice to have gotten some gratitude though, instead all I got was entitlement.

Not right away though, at first, he seemed grateful, at least I think he seemed grateful to have a good woman by his side and likewise I felt the same. He wasn't perfect but he was way better than where I'd come from.

So I didn't mind the things he lacked for the moment. I knew better days were coming, he promised me that they were up ahead. When he got up on his feet he was going to take care of me. Treat me like a queen, like I deserved to be treated. That was the incentive he gave me to keep pushing.

So I figured as long as I got it, he'll have it until he actually gets it. That meant trips to the mall of course. Meals, haircuts, everything that I did for myself I had to do for him, part of it had to do with me wanting someone who matched my energy and fly. We were a couple now; we were out and about in public. How could I be cute and fly and he not be.

I remember once there was an older woman I met while I was working at Wayfield Foods. It's a grocery store chain in Georgia for those who aren't familiar. I had to be around twenty-one or twenty-two. It was before I met the devil, but I never will forget; her words haunt me to this day.

I don't know what made this woman choose me; of all people to say this to. I figured she must have been having a bad day or something. Maybe she was bitter from a relationship that had gone sour, because I can't understand why, she felt the need to give me the advice she did.

It was out the blue. I was working, there was no man around me, what possible motive she could have for picking me to pass along this advice to, is beyond me; but I will never forget her words. She said, "if you meet a man with nothing. Leave him that way. Don't fix him up."

I don't think I was seeing anyone at the time. So, I didn't know what to make of it. I just brushed it off thinking, some man must've done her in; got her walking up to random young women, offering them relationship advice they didn't ask for.

If only I had known then, that those words of wisdom; if heeded properly, would've saved me a world of regret. I know you're thinking. *Bitch I already knew that shit.* Well bitch, I didn't; and I wish I would've listened instead of brushing the shit off.

I see this shit happen way too often. So, I know I'm not the only one; but bitches like you, will never admit to it. You'll point your finger at me and make me feel like it was just me by myself. It's okay; you don't have to admit it. Your secrets safe with me.

Best friend, what I thought was the ramblings of an old bitter woman, was words of wisdom from someone who had lived the hardship. She was giving me the advice so I didn't have to go through what she went through.

It was a golden nugget of wisdom, that I should've treated as such. This was no ordinary encounter, this was prophetic.

How else could this woman have known, that just a few short years later, I would cross paths with The Devil, and he would try to suck me dry; and not in the good way either.

Like I said before, I had a real problem with warning signs, I just couldn't see them. So, when The Devil showed up on my doorstep, in need of a good woman to lift him up until he could get back on his feet and return the favor. I jumped at the chance. I told you I felt bad for the nigga.

Pretty soon he had just as many shoes and clothes as me. His haircuts were coming regularly like my hairdos. His side of the closet had grown significantly. That little duffel bag was overflowing; to the point he'd upgraded to clothes hangers' girl!

Whenever I went shopping whether he was with me or not, I always purchased him something. I didn't care if it was a pair of underwear, which coincidently happened to be the first article of clothing I ever bought him.

I remember it well because I remember seeing him one night before he climbed into bed with me and he had on the holiest pair of drawers I'd ever seen in my life; not to mention he didn't have that many either. I know what you're thinking, *bitch you still let him fuck though*. And did, shit they were holy they weren't dirty.

Hey you asked for the truth but I see now you can't handle the truth. We haven't even gotten to the meat and potatoes of this thang yet so girl just chill.

I know you're going to say I'm the only one, right? Okay yeah, keep telling yourself that. I know bitches who have overlooked far worse. I'm sure you have a couple skeletons in your closet too, mine just the ones being aired out right now.

Anyway, to sum it up. He benefited off of my sympathy, kind heart and good nature. I didn't have to do it but I did. You can fault me for it all you want; in many ways it was my fault. I should've listened to the old woman.

Ma'am, if you're still out there. If you just so happen to pick up this book. I want you to know that I finally see what you meant. Took me long enough, but I finally get it now. Although it may be too late to save me the heartache, your words of wisdom can live on in the pages of this book and possibly help the next unsuspecting young woman.

Because God knows, I had no clue of the monster I was creating or that he would turn on me the way that he did. The one I'd picked up from the gutter and shared everything I had in this world with. Literally put drawers on his ass, and he would turn around and give that same ass to me to kiss. I had no clue that nigga would turn on me worse than a rabid pit bull biting the very hand that fed him.

Father of Lies
Chapter Six

There is one thing on this earth I cannot stand, and that's a motherfucking liar. I hate them with a passion, just lying for no good reason. Can't tell the truth to save their motherfucking life. A nigga that just make up shit; coming up with everything but the truth.

A mother fucker that just pulls shit out they ass; out the woodwork. A bold faced, bald-headed ass lie. Fabricators, storytellers, Liar liar your dick is on fire ass niggas; I hate them! So imagine my disdain, when I found out that's exactly what this nigga was.

But he wasn't just a liar. This motherfucker was the king, of liars. If his mouth was open, he was telling a lie. This nigga was a liar; and the truth just wasn't in him. His entire existence was a lie. When I first found out this nigga was the father of lies, it was when he got arrested. Bear in mind, this was just the first arrest. There would be many, many more to come.

One night after I had fallen asleep early, because as you know, I had a regular job; and this nigga didn't. I awoke in the middle of the night to my phone ringing. I didn't pick it up in enough time; so, it stopped ringing.

I looked at my screen, but I didn't recognize the number. When I tried to call the number back; it didn't work. I thought it was strange, but couldn't really focus on that issue, because the bigger, more pressing problem at the time; was that when I fell asleep, the nigga was in the bed with me. However, when I woke up, he was gone.

Forgetting about the missed phone call for the time being, I got up to check around my apartment to see where he was. I mean he had to be there, where else would he be? I checked the entire apartment; keep in mind, it was only two bedrooms. It was empty, he was gone. I looked out the window and noticed my car was gone too.

Now, two things irritated me about this scenario. One, where the fuck did he have to go in the middle of the night? Two, why the hell did he take my car, knowing full well he didn't have any license.

I wait up for a while, because at this time I can't go back to sleep. I planned to wait up until he came back, so I could curse his ass out. However, I wouldn't get the chance. The next time he walked through that door, would be months from now.

He'd gotten arrested driving my car without a license; going to get weed. So, he said. I knew that was a lie, he may have gotten weed, don't get me wrong; but I believe he left for more than just weed. The same way he left the white girl and would end up at my house in her car, that's what the nigga was doing, I could feel it.

Before I started dressing him in designer clothing, and insisting he visited the barbershop regularly. No one was thinking about this nigga. I really wish I had listened to that old lady.

Not because I didn't want him to better himself or grow. But because if he was going to switch up, at least it wouldn't feel like such a betrayal; if he built himself up, instead of me.

Eventually, an hour or so later the phone rang again. This time, I answered it on time.

"Collect call from Dekalb county jail, do you accept?"

"yes"

"Baby?"

The nigga had the nerve to baby me.

"yeah"

"Man, I got locked up."

No shit nigga.

"What happened?"

"I was driving to get some weed."

"Never mind we can talk about it later."

"Why you say that? I know you mad at me baby, don't be mad."

"Yeah, I'm mad, but we're not going to discuss all that over the phone."

"Oh yeah, you're right."

"Why didn't you wake me up, so that I could take you where you wanted to go?"

"I knew you had to work in the morning. I didn't want to wake you up." I'm sure that wasn't the reason, the nigga had disturbed my rest on many occasions. But this wasn't the time to call out his bullshit. Who the fuck wants to hear that, when you're sitting in the county? So, I let that lie slide. Fatal mistake. Never let a bitch nigga slide doing bitch ass shit.

"Where's my car?"

"They impounded it, you have to call and see which one they took it to."

"You have one-minute remaining"

"We got one-minute left."

No shit nigga.

"I'll call later to see what your bond is."

"I think I have a warrant from another county, and this might violate my parole."

It was no think; he knew he had a warrant from another county. The one Becky lived in. Hell, hath no fury like a white woman scorned.

The phone call ended. I hung up and went back to sleep. It was still very early and there was nothing I could do at the time.

When the morning came, I called my cousin and had her take me to get my car out of the impound. When I got home, he called me again. This call wasn't a free one, but I'd put money on the phone while I was out; so that I could accept his calls.

While we were on the phone talking, he asked me to call his grandmother for him and inform her, that he had been arrested. He told me to tell her, that he'd turned himself in.

I was more than willing to call his grandmother for him. The only people in his family that I'd met at the time were his mother, brother and sister. Since I'd never met or spoken to his grandmother. I looked forward to it. As best as I could under the circumstances.

However, the only thing was that I didn't want to lie to her. It irritated me that was the first thing he resorted to. He didn't even try the truth. He was a grown, twenty-three-year-old man. It wasn't like she was going to whip his ass or anything. So why the lie? Just a pathological mess.

Still, I did as he asked me to and broke my no lying rule for him; because it was his wishes, and his grandmother. It still hadn't dawned on me the type of person I was dealing with, until I spoke to his grandmother. She was polite enough over the phone. I didn't have any issues when talking to her; except for when I told her the lie, he asked me to tell.

"Your grandson asked me to tell you, that he's been booked into the Dekalb County jail. He turned himself in."

Now, his grandmother had heard of me; but she'd never met me, or spoken to me before. So, when I passed along his little message; she sort of laughed and said in a matter-of-fact tone.

"He turned himself in, huh?" Then came the scoff. "Tell him; he can't lie to me, honey."

She said emphasizing the word me. So, if he couldn't lie to her; who the fuck could he lie to? The way that she said "honey", was sort of in a mocking way. Like she knew what type of liar this nigga was, and why wouldn't she? She raised him. It's like she was trying to warn me. Someone should've told her that I don't heed warnings too well.

The conversation with his grandmother, though short; had confirmed all of my suspicions; and corroborated all the circumstantial evidence against him.

This man was a pathological liar. I knew it; he knew it; she knew it; his whole fucking family, probably knew the shit.

That was the first indication that this nigga was a liar. The second one came, when a pack of Velvet Remy hair went missing from my bathroom cabinet.

I don't care who you are on this planet. Whatever race, religion, nationality or creed you pledge. Everyone knows how important a black woman's hair is to her. Whether it grew out of my own head, or if I purchased it in-store. Bitch, I bought it; it's mine.

Another thing about me is; I don't like people touching my shit. Needless to say, I wasn't too pleased when my hair came up missing. I was even more pissed when I found out what really happened to it.

I'd had the hair for a while. I planned to do my hair with it. As I mentioned earlier; I'm a stylist. I was waiting to put it in on my next hairstyle. The hair much like all my other beauty products were in my bathroom.

The only people that lived in the apartment, was me and him, so I felt no need to put away anything I considered to be of any sort of value. My motherfucking hair was no exception.

One night, after a long day at work; I came home to find him there already. Typical shit, nothing too out of the ordinary. Where else would a motherfucker with no job be?

You can tell when a motherfucker has just been up to no good. I didn't know right away what it was, but something about that night just seemed off; from the moment I walked through the door.

"Hey, baby"

"Hey" he responded, I didn't notice the nervous expression on his face at first.

"You been home all day?"

"Yeah."

"How did business go? Did you sell anything?"

'" I made a few sales. It was slow this morning, but it picked up when the kids got out of school."

I told you before that I am a resourceful person, right? Well, since the nigga was supposedly job searching and having a hard time due to his criminal record. I saw an opportunity for him to open up shop in our apartment, and sell candy and drinks. *Yes, bitch, I heard it too. By now it was our apartment.*

There were a lot of young children and teenagers in our neighborhood; I figured he could save them the walk to the store, and the burden of having to pay the high store prices if they shopped with him. In return we could make some money in the process. Win win for everyone; right?

Well... the devil had another plan. What started off as a small way to hustle until he started working, ended up being a steady flow of income into our household. We went from selling candy, chips and soda to children; to selling hot wing plates, fish, nachos and burgers to the entire neighborhood.

Our little apartment was booming with customers of all ages and genders. He started to get a reputation around the neighborhood, as he came in contact with more people every day

I was busy at work, doing hair. As long as he was making money I didn't mind. A few times when I was home, and in the back room; I would hear a female customer being extra friendly with him.

I didn't pay it any mind. I'm not the jealous type. I'm secure in who I am, and the value I add to the relationship. As long as you know how to conduct yourself when you're with me, we're good. I found out none of that shit meant anything to a thirsty, selfish motherfucker like him. A nigga seeking validation from anything and anybody.

I tried not to let the shit go to my head though, the fact that random girls came to my door all the time; especially while I was at work.

This was a new relationship; I wanted this one to have the trust my previous one lacked. I didn't bring any distrust or bullshit from the last nigga into it. I made sure I checked the baggage at the door.

I wanted to trust him; and why not? Hell, he could trust me. The few months he was locked up, I didn't do anything behind his back. Believe me, I had several opportunities.

A lot of them came from some of them same niggas he ran with. I wasn't like that though, and for the record, I'm still not. There are some bitches though that would've made him look just as crazy as he made them look

To me, that shit just makes everybody look crazy. However, we're not going to speculate and talk about what ifs. We're going to stick strictly to the facts. The fact of the matter is; I was straight up with the nigga, transparent, an open book. However, this nigga; was on some more shit.

"I've got to tell you something baby and please don't be mad at me, ok?"

Now when a nigga that's been giving off all these warning signs start the conversation like this, you get immediately upset no matter how calm he asks you to remain. My mind was everywhere at this point, like what the fuck was this nigga about to say?

"What is it?"

"You know that hair that was in the bathroom?"

"Hair? What hair? My Velvet Remy hair?"

Velvet Remy was an expensive and popular brand of hair at the time. (If you know, you know.)

"Yeah, I had to throw it away. Don't worry, I'll buy you some more."

"Throw it away, what do you mean you had to throw it away; what for?"

"I was using the bathroom, I knocked it down by accident, and it fell in the toilet."

Possible. It's possible, right? I mean shit; anything's possible. But something about this shit wasn't adding up.

"What was it doing up on the counter anyway? It's been under the cabinet forever."

"I was looking for something earlier, I put it up there and forgot to put it back."

So, you take out my hair for no apparent good reason, put it on the counter where you leave it. Then subsequently knocks it into the toilet which happens to be filled with urine? That's seems like an unlikely series of unfortunate events.

Now, I said this motherfucker lied all the time, I didn't say the nigga was good at it. This shit was just too open and shut. Like the hair was gone and there was nothing that could be done about it. Something wasn't right. I could smell it. I could smell it like a mob boss could smell a rat.

I smelled a bitch.

"Why did you throw it away?"

"It had pee on it. "

"I could've washed it."

"For what; when I can just buy you some more."

I wished that nigga would stop throwing that shit around, like he had it like that. Let's not forget the money I made working at the salon helped fund his little store operation he was running; so really, I'd be buying my own fucking hair, twice. Of course that wasn't my response.

"That's just a waste of money, when I can get it out of the trash and wash it."

Now, I really didn't want the pissy hair out of the trash. I just wanted him to produce the hair so that I could see if what he was saying was true.

I don't know why I felt the need to disprove this ridiculous story it had no merit to begin with.

I started towards the kitchen where the trash bin was.

"It's not in the kitchen; I took out the trash already."

Oh, this shit just keeps getting better and better.

"Any other day, I have to beg you to take out the trash, but today; you just take it out all on your own; like you're top sanitation employee of the year or some shit."

"I didn't want it to start smelling like pee."

This nigga just had all the answers, didn't he. I wonder how long he sat in here coming up with this story. He had something for everything I said.

By now, I was pissed. This nigga was playing with me, playing in my motherfucking face. It wasn't even about the missing hair or the lies anymore. It was about what the missing hair and the lies signified.

There had been a bitch in my apartment while I was at work. A broke, dusty, thieving ass bitch at that. There had to have been; how else would you explain my missing hair.

Was it a customer?

But what would she be doing in the back of the apartment near the bathroom?

Maybe he let her use the bathroom and she just walked out with my hair.

Then I heard the little voice. You know that real bitch that lives deep down inside of me. She must've woken up when she heard the bullshit this nigga was trying to force feed me.

Bitch, stop thinking stupid shit, you just going to help the nigga lie to your ass. Tell him to get his shit and get the fuck out.

I didn't listen to her though, she wasn't as loud and ghetto as she is now. Time and this nigga's bullshit would make her that way.

Instead, I headed for the front door.

"Where are you going?"

"I'm going to the trash; to get my hair."

"Baby, I said I'll get you some more hair."

"No. I want *that* hair." I said heading for the door. The dumpster for our side of the apartments wasn't far from our building at all. It was just a few feet from where I'd parked.

He stood in front of the door this time.

"I said I'll buy you another one, why are you acting like this?"
Me? He was blaming me for tripping; like I was the one in the wrong here.

"I don't want you to buy me anything. Move, I'm going to get my hair. The trash man just came yesterday so that dumpster should be practically empty."

"So, you're going to go out there and dig around in the trash?"

"Yes, unless there's no reason for me to."

I added, challenging him to tell me the truth. Which meant he would have to tell the whole truth, and the look on his face told me he would rather *make* me another bundle of hair than do that.

He fell silent, I reached for the doorknob again.

"Don't go out there baby. Come on." He looked so stressed, like he was the one going through it.

"I'm going if my hair is out there; is it?" I continued to press the issue. "Is my hair out there in that dumpster or not?"

"No"

Finally, this nigga admits it.

"Where is it?"

"You're going to be mad."

It was like talking to my little nephew, and he was trying to tell me he'd done something bad but was afraid to say what it was. Only difference is, this wasn't my little nephew. This was a grown ass man and whatever bad thing he did, affected more than just him.

"I'm past mad. Where is my hair?"

"My little sister came over today" he started.

Oh, this nigga must really take me for some kind of fool.

"She had her friend with her, and she asked to use the bathroom. She must've taken your hair because when I went in there after they left it was gone."

"Why didn't you just say that?"

"I didn't want you to get mad."

"I'm mad that you lied in the first place."

"My bad baby. It was my fault; it was my sister's friend. That's why I said I would pay for it."

I'd let this nigga think he was getting somewhere with these ridiculous lies for too long. It was time to call bullshit.

"That's bullshit, your sister and her fucking friend ain't been here. You're a liar. You had a bitch in my house and she stole my hair." Then a thought that hadn't entered my mind the entire time came to me for the first time. "Did you *give* my hair to a bitch?"

"Hell no, baby I wouldn't do that."

"Then where the fuck is it?" I was yelling now. Come to think of it, this would be the same nigga that would later tell me I argue too much. Like shit like this wasn't the cause. I didn't get off work and decide to pick an argument. I had no choice; my shit was missing and he was still lying about it.

I'd like to tell you that the issue was resolved that night. Hell, I wish I could tell you that I kicked the lying no good son of a bitch out of my house; but we both know that's not what happened.

He kept lying his way around in circles. I had no proof of what really happened to the hair and till this day I never got it. That mother fucker will die with that secret on his lips. I've tried to get the truth from him about it several years later. I still get the same response. That's his story and he's sticking to it I guess.

Maybe I'll get the truth from his ass one day. Maybe he'll grant me a last dying wish.

Under his Control
Chapter Seven

One thing the devil seeks after, is complete and total control of you. There is a saying that goes around in the church community. That when you see someone acting out, you'd say; don't let the devil use you like that.

That's how I felt. I was no longer in control. The devil was using me, against me; to destroy myself. The diabolical part of it, was that he deceived me into believing that it was love.

That I was doing these things that I wouldn't normally do, all in the name of love. He had me spellbound. Had to be some sort of witchcraft, or sorcery; to make me behave the way that I did. What else would one expect from the devil.

I had put him before everyone else, including myself. *Not God though friend, I'd never put anyone before God.* Everyone else though, was counted out. All in the hopes, that there would be some type of reward of a fairytale life with him; that would never come.

He dangled that shit over my head, like you would a toy over a child's. No matter how high the child jumps, and no matter how close she gets to the prize. The person dangling the toy will only extend it further from her grasp. It is a fruitless unattainable goal.

The wise children, who realize the person never intends for them to reach the toy in the first place; give up, and go find something else to play with.

Then there's those determined, ADHD having, Ritalin dependent children, who won't or can't stop trying. They want that particular toy that's been dangling in front of them.

Whatever the reason may be. Whether they believe they deserve it because they've been trying so hard for so fucking long or whether they just don't have the fucking common sense to know; that the person holding the thing over their head, never intended to give it to them from the fucking beginning.

Yet they stay and continue to jump for the shit. Until, the people around witnessing the constant failure each time they jump up; just to come crashing back down with nothing to show for their efforts. Can't help but think, the bitch must be crazy. Why won't she stop?

Doesn't she see that he's going to keep pulling it back no matter how close she gets.

That was me friend. This nigga was toying with me. Dangling this life that he knew he didn't want with me over my head. I played the game to the

end. I played by the rules. Did
everything he asked. How did I still
lose? He wanted me to jump, I didn't
ask how high, I just aimed for the
sky. No matter how high I soared. He
would always pull back.

Do you know how many years it
took me to figure out that I was right
where the motherfucker wanted
me? Under his spell. This wasn't me
friend. I'm beautiful always have
been. I mean, I may not take home first
place in the Miss Universe pageant but I
can be runner up. Yeah, runner up
might be a stretch too, but bitch I bet
you I could be on that stage...cleaning it
after the show is over. What the fuck
ever bitch, I look good is the point. I
don't need validation from the whole
fucking universe!

The real flex is that beauty isn't my
only strong suit. I'm also ambitious,
creative and smart. You're reading my
work; you see the skills. I've always
been an intelligent person. I've done

some stupid shit before (I mean haven't we all?) but I'm not stupid by a long shot. I have a keen intellect and if you don't think so google the word intellect. I'll wait.

Yep, me all day friend.

So, how does a person with my obvious sense of self-awareness; drop the ball on this one. I'll tell you how. Love, plain and simple. That's what he used to control me; the love I had for him. Nothing else. You could say I was a willing participant, but anyone who's ever been controlled by love will tell you differently.

You know the smart thing to do, the right thing to do; but love can have you doing the complete opposite. Show me a person that has never done anything crazy in the name of love, and I'll show you a person that's never been in love.

Love makes you do crazy shit. It makes you think crazy shit, say crazy shit and act like a crazy bitch. I was the kind of crazy in love with this man that Bey sang about. Hopelessly, relentlessly and dangerously in love. Crazy in love like blue face and Chrisean. How do you rid yourself of that type of love? You don't. Don't you think if I could've; I would've?

I knew the motherfucker meant me no good from the beginning; I knew it, I had to have known it. If I hadn't been going through the shit I was going through with my ex I would've seen it. They say the devil tends to come in when you're at your lowest point. I should've saw the shit coming. I really should have friend.

I know you're probably thinking. *Bitch, if it was so bad, why did you stay?* I ask myself that question everyday friend. It wasn't all bad, at least not in the beginning. When we first got together, it was a lot going on. My brother had fallen ill, I was fighting this nigga's legal battles and my ex was stalking us, or should I say me rather. I remember thinking if we could just get past this, we'll be good. But there was always something coming up that we would need to get past, and we just never made it to good. The devil was the cause of ninety-nine percent of our problems and the other one percent came from other contributing factors.

I need to jump back for a minute, because I failed to mention that in the beginning the devil and I didn't come together as harmoniously as you thought. My ex, the one I told you who didn't leave without a fight. When he found out the devil and I were living together, that nigga put up one hell of a fight.

He would call my phone every day to try and get back together with me, and when that wouldn't work he resorted to just harassing me and cursing me out. When I stopped answering his calls, he would leave threatening voicemails; and the threats weren't necessarily just for me either. He didn't just stop there. He would show up to the apartment we lived in together. I had to call the cops on him on numerous occasions. Whenever we would go somewhere he would show up to pick a fight with us.

Once we were at my cousin's house and my ex showed up. He was hell bent on getting inside and getting his hands on the devil. When he couldn't get him to come outside, he decided to take his wrath out on my car. It got so bad that my cousin who my ex was actually cool with; had to intervene and tell him that she wasn't going to stand there and allow him to destroy her cousin's car in front of her house.

He was in her driveway vandalizing my vehicle, something he would do on multiple occasions; whenever he came across my car parked somewhere. He wanted us to come out of my cousin's house to confront him.

Eventually, with that type of erratic behavior going on, like any man would; the devil suggested we get a gun for protection. That; along with the fact that he'd turned his small candy business to a one stop shop for all the quintessential hood needs; such as alcohol, cigarettes, blunts and various other recreational essentials. You name it, he sold it.

If only someone would've told me that the only person, I needed protection from was him. My ex's idle threats paled in comparison to the ones the devil would later impose.

If you would've told me at the time I allowed him to bring that gun in my home; that I'd be the one staring down the barrel of it. I would've told him hell no; we don't need it.

Who am I kidding? When the hell was I able to tell this nigga no? Better yet, when the hell did he ever ask for permission to do anything. I'm convinced this nigga was working some kind of witchcraft, voodoo or black magic to keep me under this kind of control.

You don't understand, there was no reasoning with me at this point. I was no longer operating under my own volition. I was completely under his control.

The more control he asserted, the worse he became. The more I grew his image and style, the more he grew in popularity in the neighborhood and ultimately; with thirsty ass hoes. Old woman if you're reading, I know you're shaking your head at me; like I told this bitch.

It was too late, by now he was unrecognizable as the humble man I'd met and fell in love with. He definitely looked better and I was happy about that but he wasn't behaving any better. The more I poured into him and built him up, the worse he treated me. Like how the fuck does that even work? The shit doesn't make sense. Normal people don't repay good with evil.

Manipulation and control disguised to look and feel like love. I can hear your judgmental ass now. *Bitch, you let him do it.* Bitch, didn't I say this was no ordinary nigga? This was the devil! Satan, The evil one. Ruler of demons. When it came to deception this nigga was the master.

Master of deception
Chapter Eight

I told you that nigga was the father of lies already, right? What I haven't told you yet though, was that this nigga was also the master of deception. Nothing with this nigga was ever what it seemed. This nigga had everyone fooled.

I believe, that we all have; at one time or another in our lives, lived a lie. Don't think so? Ok, take out your wallet, and pull out your driver's license. Now check under the little section where it says weight. See; a lie.

Don't feel bad though, this nigga was living about fifty, simultaneously. I would've diagnosed him with multiple personality disorder, if he had any personality at all to begin with. Unfortunately for him, being a liar isn't' a personality trait.

You just didn't know what you were waking up to each day. When you went to bed, you had a lover and a protector. When you woke up, you had a companion, a soul mate to share your life with. By the afternoon, when his friends came around you had a thug a gangster; a rapper, a ruthless, candy selling, nacho plate making kingpin and behind your back with bitches this nigga was living life as a single man.

He pretended to be so many things to so many people with so little consistency that nobody knew the essence of who this nigga truly was but me and I don't think I one hundred percent knew.

The bravado demeanor he possessed at the liquor store hadn't quite left after all.□ It was still there, lying dormant.□ I learned the hard way that when he didn't have any friends around, he had no one to put on a presentation for.☐ However, that would change as soon as they showed up.☐

He would act like Nino fucking Brown or some shit.☐ It was just an over show of dominance, like he owned me.☐ It was truly a spectacle to behold.☐ I remember watching him go from my man to an asshole in a matter of seconds.☐ The shit was almost comical and I would've laughed too if the shit wasn't happening to me.☐

It didn't just stop at his friends either, his family, hell even mine; the motherfucker didn't care.☐ I think what he lacked in masculinity, as far as being the provider and protector; he would overcompensate for with brute☐force, control and authority.☐ It's like he wanted everyone to know that he was in fact the man of the house and in complete control; in case there were any doubts.

I heard a wise woman once say, that you have to pay the cost if you want to be the boss. ☐

Another thing he would do is he would always accuse me of talking to and treating him like a "child" then would turn around and do the most childish shit. ☐ If by child, he meant that I took care of his ass; then yes, I would have to agree. ☐ If you want to be treated like a man you need to act accordingly, am I right? ☐

The first thing most men say, is if you act like a hoe then that's what you're going to be treated like. ☐ Well, the shoe should still fit right?

Not working, sitting at home eating snacks and playing video games all day, sounds like childish behavior to me. ☐ However, I'm expected to look the other way and still talk to and treat you like a man. ☐ You know not what you ask, that is a hard thing to ask of *any* woman. Damn near impossible. That type of willful ignorance isn't easy.

Still, I achieved it with top tier performance all the same.□ He exhibited no manly behavior in my home whatsoever; with the exception of providing dick of course and I still treated him like he was the King of my castle. □ Talk about mother fucking unwavering commitment.□

Even with all of that I had no idea what I was in store for. When I tell you nothing with this nigga was as it seemed. I remember once he told me he was going to New York, something to do with his rap career or lack thereof. Before then he'd never flown before.

He took luggage and everything, I believe I even helped the nigga pack; went and bought travel toiletries and shit. I assisted him with his travel arrangements in every way that I could; everything but the actual flight arrangement of course but everything else I made sure he was good to go.

This was his first flight; he was nervous which could be expected for anyone's first time flying. Hell, I was nervous for him. At that time, neither of us had traveled by air before. I was proud to see my man opening up new traveling ventures for us. It would make it easier for me to step outside of my own comfort zone and get over my fear of flying. I couldn't have been more proud of him. That was until he left and came back.

If memory serves me correctly, I do remember that he came back much earlier than expected. He said they'd gotten done a day or two earlier and they ended up coming home early. I didn't think anything of it. I mean why should I have? The bigger question that begs to be answered is why would an adult fabricate a story about leaving the state?

It wouldn't be until nearly two years later that I would find out the whole trip to New York act was some bullshit. One day he actually had a flight to Texas come up and we were discussing his trip. Here my helpful ass was again getting ready to see the nigga off and out the blue the nigga says.

"I'm already nervous, you know I've never flown before." and I look at the nigga and say.

"I'm nervous, baby."

"Why?"

"You know I've never flown before."

So you can Imagine me pausing mid-pack mind, you with the freshly washed and folded socks and drawers I just laundered for the nigga still in my hands and I look at his ass and say.

"But you flew to New York."

"When?"

"A couple years ago."

"I've never flown to New York." He dismissed what I said without so much as glancing in my direction.

"Yes, the fuck you did."

"No, the fuck I didn't baby. I would remember if I fucking went to New York." He said getting annoyed.

"You did! You told me a whole fucking story about taking your shit through customs and everything."

"I ain't never told you I flew to New York. Man, get the fuck out of here. You're tripping."

I was flabbergasted. I couldn't believe this nigga.

"Are you serious?"

"Man, watch out. I'm trying to get ready to go on a trip and you're just trying to start shit with me.

"Are you fucking kidding me right now? Are you serious?"

"Are you serious?" He said treating me like I was a mental patient or some shit. He had lied to me, made up this whole fucking story and now it was clear by the look on his face that he'd forgotten the extravagant lie he'd told to disappear for the weekend. He'd told so many lies he couldn't keep up with them.

It was evident the type of liar and manipulator I'd gotten myself mixed up with. There was no time to get into it and pick apart the nigga's two-year-old lie because he had a flight to catch for real that time, I hope. So, I was forced to drop the subject. Which even after he returned home he continued to deny he ever flew to New York.

By this time, you would've thought I knew what type of gas lighting, narcissist I was dealing with, but every time I thought I knew the full extent of this man's deception and manipulation this nigga kept upping the ante.

I mentioned that I had sympathy for him and I did sometimes. He would tell sob stories about his upbringing and his absent father. He made it seem like he had the worst childhood. Now, I don't even know if it was true or if it was just another deceptive practice he used to gain sympathy.

How likely are you to correct or hold accountable someone you pity? It was like letting a troubled child get away with stuff because you didn't want to punish them. You'd feel bad if you brought anymore trauma or pain to their life. You don't stop to think about the trouble or pain they'll bring to yours; if left uncorrected.

Don't get me wrong, I tried to get out before things took a bad turn, but by this time I was up to my knees in bullshit. Around the time my brother fell ill, there were times when he had long stays in the hospital and his children would stay with me until he came home.

One day I came home from work and my brother's children who were all very young at the time, around the age of ten and under; they told me that he'd had some people over and they were playing cards. No big deal, right? Well, depends on who the fuck came over.

A little inside history about us is that we love card games. Poker, spades, you name it, we play it. We used to always host spade games at the apartment so it wasn't a huge shock that he would host a game. Whenever we played spades he and I were always on the same team. We were a hard duo to beat on a spades table.

However, this time the nigga was pulling one of those disrespectful ass moves he liked to pull and expected me not to say any fucking thing. Even the children knew this nigga had lost his fucking mind because as soon as I got home; the first thing they told me, was he made them stay in the back room, while they played spades. No big deal, they had no business around adults playing cards anyway.

However, it would be my niece that informed me that he had a girl on his team. It wasn't supposed to be a girl in my house, let alone on his fucking team. That was it! I'd had enough of this nigga's shit. When he came back through that door, I was putting him and his shit the fuck out. I was done with his ass. I was in our room sitting on the bed, when he walked back through the front door. I didn't get mad, I didn't even raise my voice, I was just done with the bullshit at this point friend.

I called him to the back room, and wasted no time telling him that he had to get his stuff and leave. That he had no business having any bitches in my house when I wasn't home; period. He started lying saying the girl came in to buy something while they were playing cards and she happened to sit down in the chair while he got her purchase together.

My niece said the bitch was playing cards on his team like she'd seen me play with him. This nigga was a liar. You might say it's possible that she sat down for a second at the exact time my niece came out, but I think the bitch was there playing with his ass the entire time. Believe who you want to believe, I'm rolling with baby girl on this one; so that nigga had to go.

Once I gave him the rundown and told him what it was; the nigga started acting like he was the victim. He starts to argue that he hasn't done anything wrong and that I was tripping and I was always looking for reasons to leave him, like *he* wasn't the one giving me the reason to want to leave.

I wasn't hearing it this time though friend, the shit was disrespectful. In my house, in front of my brother's children; like hell no, I'm not going. So I refused to listen to his lies this time, I told him it was over. Like I said, I was sitting on the bed. By the time he'd come back home, it was dark outside; the sun had gone down.

Seeing that I wasn't going to be so easily convinced of his bullshit this time and that my foot was firmly planted. He could feel himself slowly losing control. I didn't give no fucks, not one. I was standing on business this time, his lying ass had to go. Friend, you would've been real proud of me that day. Hell, I was proud of myself at the moment.

That was; until he bit down on his jaw and walked silently over to the closet. I was expecting him to grab his duffel bag down and start packing his shit; instead he reached up and pulled the 9mm handgun down from the shelf. I didn't panic right away because I thought he was taking it down to pack it up along with the rest of his shit; but the devil had another plan.

The nigga walked over to the light switch and flicked the shit off.

"What are you doing? Turn the light back on." I said immediately standing to my feet.

Without the light, the room was pitch black. He didn't respond he just stood there with his back against the wall, blocking both the door and the light switch. He was knowingly, preventing me from leaving the room.

"What are you doing, turn on the light." I repeated, deathly afraid. I couldn't see a thing, not even him and he was only a couple of feet in front of me. All kinds of shit was going through my mind. My brother's children were in the next room and their safety was my top concern.

Who would've thought that telling him to leave, after all the disrespectful shit he'd done; that he would react like this. I felt like the nigga was begging me to break up with him, daring me to end the shit; so I did. I didn't expect this would be his reaction. For someone that acted like he had so many fucking options; this behavior to a break up was extreme.

"Turn on the light". I begged trying to remain calm. If he was at the edge I didn't want to be the one to push him over.

"No," he responded coldly. His tone had no warmth or feeling whatsoever. Who was this? This couldn't be the same man; not my man?

"I'm serious turn it on." I said now trying to reach behind him to get to the light switch or the door knob.

"Move, don't touch me." He said swiping my hand away. He knew damn well I had to go through him to get to either.

When he pushed my arm away, I could feel the gun he had gripped tightly in his hand. I went for the door knob again.

"Get off me, don't touch me." He warned.

"Turn on the light, you're scaring me!" I said about to cry now, because bitch; how the fuck was I going to get out of this room and get my brother's children out of the house.

The man I thought I knew was gone. I didn't know who this nutcase was or why he was acting like this. I started to wonder if I even knew him at all. Maybe that bad childhood he talked about had done more damage than I realized.

"So, I don't care, you keep trying to leave me for nothing."

"No, I don't". I said hoping to calm him down.

"Yes, you do."

This went on for a while. After finally calming him down and coming to an understanding, that till this day; I still don't understand why he didn't leave that night.

I was however, allowed to leave the room he had me barred in. I can't really say he held me at gunpoint; because he didn't point the gun at me. Not that day anyway. He just held it in his hand but the shit was still terrifying and intimidating.

All that and that nigga was the one in the wrong.

The things he would get away with doing to me, I couldn't dare do to him. One day some of the same people he would go next door to play cards with at their house, had invited me over to play with them. They'd been over to our house before and I played with them but I never went over to their house. So, one night when he wasn't home they invited me.

I can't remember where he was, your guess is as good as mine. However, when he came home later that night, my friend and I were at our apartment chilling. I don't remember what she said verbatim or how she said it. All I remember is that she mentioned us going over to the house to play cards. Keep in mind, there were both male and females present, so I didn't see what the problem was.

Before I knew what happened the nigga slapped my face. I couldn't remember if it was backhanded or what all I know is that the shit stung and I didn't even go to the fucking house, I was only considering going. He then proceeded to yell.

"Don't even think about going over there! Let me hear that you went over there and see what happens." He threatened.

I was shocked, I'm like nigga; what the fuck is the problem? You take your ass over there whenever you want to. Truthfully it wasn't even my type of crowd and I had no desire to go to begin with; however, the fact that he went but didn't want me to go, looked suspicious as fuck. Like nigga; what are you hiding?

"What's the matter with me going over there? You go all the time whenever you feel like it, besides him and his girlfriend come over here to play cards sometimes too." Normally when they came to my house it was just the couple but at their house they had a gang of people there.

"Fuck around and find out then."

Now, I know the nigga had no business putting his hands on me, period; no matter what the situation was. Believe it or not, I'm a tough girl, and a fighter too. All that shit means nothing when you're deceived into thinking you're in love. You don't want to fight the one you love; (even though the nigga clearly had no problem putting his hands on me,) you don't want to risk hurting them or having to call the police or none of that shit.

I didn't immediately think of it as abuse because it was just a slap. He wasn't kicking my ass or anything. It wasn't a punch to the face. If it would've had a little more power behind it, it would've knocked me off my feet. It's a good thing he hit like a bitch. It was more like a love tap between girlfriends or slap your sister would give you, if the two of you got into a squabble.

So, I let the nigga off the hook with a warning to keep his hands to himself. Fatal mistake number two. Never, and I mean never; let a fuck nigga slide with fuck shit. They get away with that shit once; they're going to try it again. It's only a matter of time.

Try it again; he did. The fact that this nigga wasn't being hard checked on none of the bull shit he was doing; had him feeling like he was invincible. He had bitches calling his phone, pretending they were calling to see if the store was open. When I confronted him about it, he was like everyone has my number.

That part was true, for plate orders they were allowed to call ahead and place their orders so it would be ready by the time they came to pick it up. Some people would also call to see if we were home or when we'd be open. Giving out the phone number wasn't my idea, but he insisted it made business easier.

I couldn't prove the shit, but it was definitely more to it than just placing orders or checking to see if we were open. I remember answering the phone and a bitch would hang up. Like I couldn't take an order or something. Hoes were playing on the phone and this nigga was playing in my face.

If I got upset or said anything about the shit, then I was accused of wanting to argue. I was seen as the one that was tripping, like he wasn't doing what he was clearly doing. Deceived into believing the shit wasn't what it obviously was.

By that time, I was tired friend, Hell, I'm getting exhausted just thinking about the shit. So, I stopped giving a fuck and started going out to get away from the house. I figured that would keep down arguments and confusion, the less time we spent together.

I left my own home to get a peace of mind, away from him and his business that he ran out of it. He was always home so if I wanted peace, I had to leave to find it.

One night, I decided to go out to get away from the house. I called my friend to come pick me up. You know, the same one who let the beans spill about us going to the neighbors card game.

We ended up going out and having some drinks. We hung out for a while, a long while. Before we knew it, time had gotten away from us. We weren't doing anything crazy, we were just hanging out together. I'd been spending a lot of time catering to the devil That I hadn't been as present in my other relationships like I used to be.

So, she kept me out late, pretty late. The sun didn't beat me home or no shit like that, but that nigga had stayed out late with his friends before too, so I didn't think it was going to be a big deal.

The devil had another plan.

When she dropped me off, I was beyond wasted. I could barely get my key in the door. I was struggling with the key and the lock, when the door was suddenly and violently snatched open.

"Where the fuck have you been?"

He said pulling me into the apartment and slamming the door shut behind us. "Do you know what fucking time it is?"

I was trying to keep my balance and make my way to the back of the apartment so I didn't have to hear his hypocritical ass mouth. Like I'm supposed to be cool when he does it, but when I do it, it's a problem.

"Where have you been?" He asked again angrily.

The more I tried to feel my way through the dark apartment the more shit I bumped into and knocked over.

"What's wrong with you?"

He asked unaware that I was inebriated when he answered the door.

He finally turns on the lights and see that I can barely stand or keep my eyes open. Even I didn't know I'd had that much to drink. When I was riding in the car on the way home, it didn't seem like I'd had that much.

However, when I started walking around shit got difficult. Anyway that nigga was always hanging out late smoking weed and drinking with his friends so the shit shouldn't have mattered.

"Oh, so you a drunk bitch?" He realized surprised. "Ok; so you want to go out and do hoe shit." He said with a sinister laugh. "I got you, wait right there."

He runs to the back of the apartment and disappears into our bedroom. When he emerges I could see him holding the shiny metal chrome handgun at his side. When I lifted my eyes up to see his face it was contorted in an evil demonic scowl. There was nothing cute about it anymore.

I tried to gain some sympathy from him by looking into his eyes but there was none there for me, all I could see was darkness until he raised the gun up to my face and I saw the light. The light reflecting off of the chrome finish that is.

He grabbed me by the hair and pulled my head back pushing the muzzle of the gun up against my cheek hard

"Where the fuck have you been huh? Where the fuck have you been?"

He yelled. I could feel saliva flying from his mouth into my face.

During the struggle some kind of way I ended up on the ground. He could've knocked me over with a feather as uncoordinated as I was. He then knelt down putting the gun to my head first.

"You think I'm playing with you? The next time I ask you where the fuck you been? You better fucking answer me" He said pressing the gun harder against my face

"Nowhere." I said trying to push my face out of the path of the gun and or bullet.

"Naw, you been somewhere, where the fuck you was at, and why you couldn't answer your fucking phone huh?"

He mushed the muzzle of the gun against my temple, I could feel the cold steel pressing against my skin. I was drunk but I was still scared shitless. I was just waiting to hear the sound of the gun go off. It didn't cross my mind that he would intentionally pull the trigger, I just thought with me pushing his hand and him trying to put the gun to my head that it would accidentally go off.

So, I tried not to keep struggling so much over the gun. I just kept saying "leave me alone" and "get off me" loudly.

"Shut the fuck up." He said attempting to stick the gun into my mouth.

The Road to Hell
Chapter Nine

That was the moment I realized that I was headed down the wrong road. You remember that song Highway to Hell by AC/DC? *Oh, okay so I'm the only black girl that listens to rock n roll?* I'm sure you've heard it, at least on a movie soundtrack, it's been on plenty of them.

Well, if you've ever heard the song; then you'll know that's exactly how I felt at that moment. I could hear the lyrics playing in my head as I stared up at the sinister look in his eyes, while he tried desperately to get me to open my mouth; so he could fit the barrel of the pistol in it.

"I'm on a highway to hell."

"Highway to hell."

All I could think was, what if it goes off? Then what huh?

This was the gangster side that was meant for his friends and the general public but here he was using it on me.

The master of deception had gotten his personas mixed up. I was supposed to be getting the loving and caring side. What I should've known was that he had no loving side and he didn't care.

I fought back until he stopped. He was still angry but by now so was I. This was the second time this motherfucker had grabbed that gun when he was angry with me and it wouldn't be his last. I've never seen this nigga pull that shit on anyone but me since he had it. I was starting to believe he bought the shit for me, and to think I helped the nigga pay for it.

Friend, if I'm being honest and I am. I can't really remember how that night ended for us. I know the arguing and the tension subsided. The nigga probably slept in the same bed as me after the shit happened.

I blamed myself, thinking I'd made him jealous and it was my fault, If I'd been at home where I was supposed to be, it would've never happened. Instead of having him change his controlling, possessive, erratic behavior.

I adjusted my actions, and became this completely submissive, subservient person. In hopes that I wouldn't arouse those types of reactions from him. I mean you'd do anything to not have a gun pointed in your face, right? I'd find out soon enough that it didn't matter how "good" I was; this nigga was just plain evil.

Did getting rid of him ever cross my mind? Of course it did. I tried on more than one occasion. There was a small part of me that was afraid to see that decision all the way through.

There was a time when we broke up and he actually left the apartment. I was in the car with my friend when he called me and told me that he was going to off himself. Insinuating it was because of the break up. You see the types of mind games this nigga be playing. I don't even think he'd been gone longer than 48 hours.

But being the compassionate person that I am, I was concerned. My friend however wasn't as convinced. She was like,

"Hang up, he's just saying that. If he was going to kill himself, he wouldn't call you first. He'd just do it."

"Of course I didn't want him to kill himself, her assurance did nothing to ease my conscious. I tried to help him before hanging up the call. I told him to relax and call his family and talk to them; but the next words out the niggas mouth were disturbing to say the least.

"I don't want to talk to anyone, I'm tired of being here. I'm tired of dealing with bullshit."

"Why are you saying this?"

"Because I am, I'm going to kill myself tonight."

"Don't do that, you need to call your grandma them."

"Nope, for what? Don't nobody care about me."

"Yes, people do."

"No, they don't. I'm going to kill myself tonight…….. and I'm taking you with me."

Just crazy shit. Did I believe he would do it?

At the time I don't know what I believed. Threatening my life had become a routine method of control for him. I remember another break up where I got him to leave, he was gone longer this time for over a week I think. I was done friend like really done. I wasn't even accepting his phone calls so he couldn't call and threaten me.

I remember I was at work with my same friend. He walked in my job, by this time I was working at a financial institution so I was behind a protective bullet proof glass. When he came to the window, I didn't talk to or acknowledge him. I just got up, walked to the back and stayed out of his sight until he left. I ignored him right in front of everyone.

I think that's what made him the angriest. He didn't like to be ignored. While I was in the back trying to avoid him, he left. Once he was gone a text came through to my phone. When I opened it, it was the picture of a man I didn't recognize. I was confused, so I walked over to my friend to show her the picture. I said "He text me this picture of some guy."

I thought he was accusing me of being involved with the guy and this was his way of confronting me. I never expected to hear the next words that came out of my friend's mouth as she was the one to recognize who the person on the picture was.

"Girl, just answer the phone and talk to that man."

The phone was ringing again.

"Why?"

I was confused because this was my same friend who'd told me to ignore him when he threatened to harm himself, the last time we broke up.

Now she was telling me to pick up the phone for him. I could tell the image disturbed her but I didn't know why. I've never been one to sit and scroll on social media platforms so there was no way I'd have known who the person on the picture was; until she explained it to me.

"Girl, that's the man that went live on social media and started shooting people because his girlfriend dumped him and wouldn't talk to him."

"What?" I asked shocked he would send me a picture of someone who would do that. The message was loud and clear.

"Yeah, he just walked up to this old man, shot him and said to the camera that it was her fault." My friend continued explaining.

Aggressive controlling behavior at the highest level. God only knows why the relationship lasted as long as it did because I sure don't. He would say or do the most fucked up shit; then would want to carry on like the shit never happened. He never wanted to take accountability for his actions. I had to just be willing to forgive him.

It was very confusing too because after he'd do some fucked up shit, and girl; he was really doing some fucked up shit. He would do something nice, kind and loving. Roses, gifts, dates, romance and romantic gestures would follow and it would all run together to where it felt like, this was love.
Fuss, fight, fuck, then forgive.
Fuss, fight, fuck, then forgive; and not necessarily in that order either.

It was a cycle that happened so frequently that it just became normal.

No one outside of my immediate friends knew what was going on inside my house. Co-workers and family saw the roses he'd send to my job but no one knew what preceded those flowers and gifts. Those were apology presents and they hardly made up for the transgression they were intended for. This all came from the man I loved, how could I interpret it to be anything other than love? The devil had me so confused, I was on the highway to hell and didn't even know it.

They say the road to hell is paved with good intentions. Well I guess mine was paved with love and I had nothing but the best intentions for us both. I put all my efforts into procuring the perfect life for us. Everything I built, he tore down.

He didn't want the home I was trying so desperately to create here with him because he was quite comfortable in the one he had in hell. His plans were to drag me back there with him.

If only I had known that our relationship would be as hopeless as his rap career; both just going no fucking where.

Still I supported his dream, what kind of woman would I be if I didn't support the man's dream. Not that he ever gave me credit for supporting him anyway. He didn't want a woman he wanted a groupie. Don't get me wrong, I have no problem being what my man wants me to be. I do however, have a problem with being silent while I watch a nigga try to get away with bullshit in front of my face.

One night me, him and some of my friends go out to a club where he is to perform one of his songs. It was some type of open mic night or something. So we get there, order some drinks and all is fine for the first half hour to forty-five minutes.

I'd been on his social media page and saw some messages between him and this girl. I can't remember what the messages said, I just know they were messaging one another. I didn't see anything sexually explicit or anything; I don't think.

Remember, I'm not the jealous type whatsoever. However, this chick who didn't live anywhere in our area, walked into the club. His ass didn't know I went through his shit, so he thought I didn't know who the bitch was.

The moment I saw her step through the door, I went up on his ass. He really called this bitch up to the same club he had me at to watch him perform and when I checked him about it, he tried to lie and say she just showed up. He didn't ask her to come, and that he posted that he would be there performing on social media so everyone knew.

The nigga was just a fucking liar. I wish I hadn't said anything; I should've just sat there to see what the nigga really proposed to do; because what was really the purpose? Why even invite both of us? I guess the nigga just liked living on the edge, I don't fucking know.

I had no idea how close to the edge we both were about to go. Somewhere after this we went through a torrential turbulent time in our finances. Mainly because this nigga had no sense of financial responsibility or stability. Whatever he earned he spent down to the last dime. He didn't have a bank account let alone a savings account.

He didn't plan for the future, because he didn't care about the future; his or mine. It was like living with a grown child. Neither one of us had any children but please understand I was raising a man. K Michelle tried to warn me about that shit, she tried to warn a lot of us ladies. Somebody should've told K that I don't heed warning signs too well.

Here I was trying to teach this nigga, responsibility, manners, how to obtain gainful employment, how to sustain said employment. How to conduct himself, how to treat me, love me, fuck me. Shit if it wasn't for that last part you could say I had adopted a fucking man child.

That was a lot of fucking work bitch, a lot of teaching and I didn't get summers' off either. I had to do that shit year-round. I can imagine that proud feeling a teacher has when they see their pupil excel after having filled the empty vessel with knowledge and wisdom.

There must've been a crack in my vessel because I was pouring in; but the shit wasn't being retained. I guess it must've leaked out the crack of his ass or something; I don't know. I just know the information didn't retain; message wasn't received.

Our downward spiral came from this nigga's poor management of money and his inability to stay out of the judicial system. He had been arrested so many times I'd practically funded the local police department through expensive jail phone calls, paid bonds and money for commissary.

Nearly ten arrests in ten years and if I wanted to skip a visitation from being tired of seeing jail corridors the nigga would act like I was the one in the wrong. He would accuse me of not loving him or caring for him or being there for him. Truth was, I was just tired of the back and forth jail shit.

The day I realized I hadn't left my ex and my past behind as far as I thought I had, came as quite the shock. I found out just how much my future love had in common with my past one one morning when I was sitting in court with him. He had to answer for not complying with his probation. I was there for no other reason other than comfort and moral support. I didn't know that by the time court was over, I would be the one in need of comfort and support. My simple ass was about to get a rude awakening.

I thought I'd leveled up like Ciara, thought I'd found my Russell Wilson child. I had no idea that the future I'd so carefully and meticulously planned out was more bleak than before.

The judge asked him why hadn't he been complying with probation and why he wasn't working. The nigga ran off a list of lies like he usually does but unfortunately for him the judge wasn't new to that shit he was true to it. He wasn't going to just go for whatever he said.

After listening to him try to lie his way out of the situation the judge finally spoke.
"Okay Mr. Lucifer. (No, he didn't actually call him that I'm just paraphrasing but I'm sure that's what he meant.) You say you start your new

job on Monday; that's good. I'm willing to allow you to go home but first I'm going to ask that you take a drug test before you leave. If it's negative than you are free to go, if it isn't I'm afraid you'll be staying for ninety days."

Imagine my surprise when he came from the back with his probation officer, after having taken the drug tests and the judge announces that he tested positive for the same drugs my ex was on. I can see my ex now somewhere laughing it up at my ass.

He hid the shit from me, the nigga was living two completely separate lives. The cat was finally out of the bag and I saw that nigga for who he truly was. By then it was too late, he was going down fast and he was taking me with him.

When his 90 days were up we ended up having to move from our apartment and in with my brother and his four children. I was supposed to be moving forward, but with the devil in my life I found myself moving backwards. I was back in my brother's home, imposing on him and his children once again. On the bright side, my brother got the nigga a job where he worked.

On the much darker side, things were about to get tremendously worse. This much like our relationship and anything else this nigga got his hands on, he would soon find a way to destroy it.

On the Devil's territory
Chapter Ten

The road I'd taken, had led me straight to hell. I mean; where else would the devil lead you? It was official, I was on his territory now. I'd lost my apartment; was about to lose my car and I was now depending on him to get us out of the hole he'd put us both in.

I know what you're thinking; I could've left anytime I chose to. That I didn't have to take him with me to my brother's house; and you're right. I didn't. However, by now I was waist deep. I'd invested so much in this nigga, I mean this relationship and I hadn't gotten a single return on any of it.

It was like a bad investment and I was desperately trying to recover my losses instead of just cutting them altogether.

All of the time, money, effort and energy I put into this motherfucker. Had I known that over time niggas depreciated in value; I would've diversified my romantic portfolio.

Instead, I risked it all on him and he'd gone from an asset to a liability within a matter of months.

It should've dawned on me that I was better off without this nigga. In our first two years together, I'd lost everything I'd worked hard for. I was emotionally and financially bankrupt. Everything I had before I met him was gone. We even lost the storage with everything from our apartment in it.

With everything slipping away, I looked to him for support; both mentally and financially. I mean; this was supposed to be my man, my rock, my provider. It was his turn to hold me down like I had done for him for so fucking long.

Fatal mistake number three, never put your hopes in a person who gambles with their own life. While you're depending on them, they're leaving everything to chance. You should've seen how easy it was for this nigga to gamble with my money, my possessions, my livelihood; my fucking heart.

When we got to my brother's house, the plan was to stay for a few weeks; get our shit together and get our own place again. However, a few weeks turned into a few months. We paid him weekly during our stay, but as you know it isn't the same as having your own place. I wish I had known then that it would be a whole year before we got our own place again.

We didn't spend the entire year at my brother's house though, as I said we were only there a few months. The remainder of the year we were without a residence or the most commonly used term homeless. We spent that time hotel hopping.

During the time he worked at my brother's job, I was in between jobs or the most commonly used term; unemployed. Much like his length of employment, I wouldn't be unemployed for very long. I would start my next job at the financial institution I mentioned earlier. Which after six years of employment, he would get me fired from it. I'll get to that part later though.

Right now, I'm going to tell you what the nigga did at the job my brother got him. He and my brother worked on different shifts. It was known throughout the job, who the nigga was to my brother and that my brother had gotten him the job.

The very first thing this hoe ass nigga do is cozy up to this hillbilly looking ass white hoe. Now, bear in mind; that I have no issue with any race

147

be it white, black, Asian or what have you. I'm just pointing out the fact that the nigga may have had a type or a fetish; I don't know.

What I do know, is that here this nigga was again playing in the snow. Hadn't learned his lesson yet. Had been to jail and everything behind the last one. Hell, it was me and his grandmother that paid the bail, so I guess he didn't give a fuck one way or the other.

He claimed he and the girl had nothing going on. Although I had no proof, I strongly believe otherwise. Another thing the nigga would never admit to but I'm going with my gut on that one. I could feel it was more to it than what he said.

On top of frolicking around with the white hoe up at my brother's job like the nigga had no home training or common sense. He started systematically stealing from the customer's to where they found out and fired his ass.

So not only did he embarrass me up there with the white bitch, but he made my brother the person that got him the job look bad too. This nigga was a one-man wrecking crew, wreaking havoc everywhere he fucking went.

I should've known something wasn't right about this man hell nothing was right about this man when I saw that he didn't have the discipline to earn a decent living. Now when I say decent I don't necessarily mean adequate, I mean literal decency, honor, integrity, morally earning wages to consistently and securely finance our household.

Every dollar and I do mean every dollar this man has ever acquired, has not been earned legitimately. Never earned an honest day's work, never earned an honest dollar. He cheated his way through his entire life just like he did our relationship.

I must've been out of my mind to think a man with so little moral fiber, would be honest and faithful to me. He's only had two real jobs the entire decade that I knew him; he's never worked either of them more than a couple months and he stole from them both.

I watched him rip off everyone he's ever come into contact with, while I stood there believing he wouldn't do the same to me because he loved me right? Shit wrong, expect a con from a con man.

He wasn't protecting me or holding me in any type of regard. I was the slow simmering con. He had a big finale in store for me. This motherfucker would go above and beyond, I'm talking about pull out all the stops to screw over the only person that ever really had his back 1000% and do you know why, because there wasn't a shred of human decency in him from the fucking beginning.

A got damn con man is what he was, he conned his way into my heart; much like he did everything else in life. I should've known when he refused to earn an honest living that there was no integrity in this man. No respect, honor or decency; for me, himself or anyone else for that matter. These were warning signs I wish I'd paid attention to.

Hell, I wish I could fit all the hell he put me through in this story, but the fuckery is too much for this book to contain. I think it would be best expressed through motion picture. (The offer is on the table for any takers.) For now, I will give you the highlights only. The things the devil did that burned their way into my memory bank.

Like the time we were staying at one of the many efficiency lodges we'd stayed in that year.

His friend had come over and I was headed out to go visit my friend for the evening. I'd only been gone from the room for maybe twenty minutes to half an hour at the most before I had to return. He thought I was going across town a forty-five minute plus ride, and a few hours long visit, which I was; but something came up and I had to come back to the room.

I think my friend canceled on me while I was in the middle of driving over to her. I can't remember the exact reason why I came back; all I know is that I came back to the room and he and his friend looked like I had crashed the fucking party or something.

Afterwards, I remember getting a hold of his phone at some point, and I discovered that the nigga had invited some white chick he met that worked at one of the waffle houses in the area to the room. Just a trifling dirt bag piece of shit of a nigga. I confronted his bitch ass about the shit. Of course, you know he lied; shit was never what the fuck it seemed with him. He said she was looking to buy some weed. A motherfucking lie but you know that nigga wouldn't be the devil if he didn't try it.

Like I didn't know the beginning of an interracial, amateur, gangbang, porn setup when I saw one. It had all the hallmark markings of one too. A shitty hotel room, one white trash, trailer park looking ass whore; and two or more nothing ass niggas.

Our room hopping eventually took us across town as I relocated quite a bit for my job. I know, I know what you're thinking. When I left town, I should've left that nigga too right?

I almost did, especially when he started back hanging heavily with this grimy, piece of shit ass nigga he used to live with. Remember when I met him in the liquor store and I said out of the four other guys that were with him; two, I would later come to know as his brother and friend.

Well, the nigga I'm about to tell you about now is the friend. Since we'd moved in with my brother, we were back on the side of town I met him in; where he lived with his friend, his friend's girlfriend and their children.

I only met the girlfriend once or twice, we never really talked or hung out or anything. I didn't feel any type of way towards her, I just didn't take the time to get to know her. From what I could tell from the few encounters, she seemed like a sweet person.

There was a significant age difference between his friend and his friend's girlfriend. It could've been upwards of a twenty-year difference. Like she was forty-five and he was twenty-seven or some shit like that. I don't know the exact difference in their age; all I know is that she had a grown daughter somewhere around the boyfriend's age.

The daughter lived in the house with both the boyfriend and mother. Around this time, she was in her third trimester of pregnancy. Come to find out, and by come to find out I mean his bitch ass told me that the grown daughter was walking around living in her mother's house pregnant by her mother's boyfriend.

I can't make this shit up if I tried. They were all holding this huge secret from the woman. Now, do you see why I didn't want to get to know her. After learning about the no-good ass people this woman was surrounded by in life including her own daughter and the man she loved.

Being the real bitch that I am and having the one that lives down on the inside, feeding me intrusive thoughts; I wouldn't have been able to smile and be friendly in the midst of that type of betrayal and treachery.

This woman had opened up her home and her heart to this vermin of a man and he showed his appreciation and gratitude by fucking her daughter and having a child with her.

The mental state of the daughter had to be just as fucked up. What was disturbing to me however, was that he was friends with this dude. What is that saying that they say about birds who have the same feathers?

Oh yeah, them motherfuckers tend to flock together. Was this the type of betrayal and treachery I could look forward to from this nigga? He seemed unfazed around that type of Jerry Springer shit. She eventually found out and kicked both the daughter and the boyfriend bitch asses out of her house.

The two moved together and are currently raising her grandchild. Even though he and the guy remained friends, I never wanted to get to know the daughter who was around our age.

No matter how they tried to get us to hang together, I was like; hell naw, fuck that. Look what that bitch did to her own fucking mama, what the fuck do you think the hoe would do to me?

If you think that was some fucked up shit; well bitch, you ain't heard nothing yet. That was light work compared to what this nigga had in store for my ass.

So, when we moved away from my brother's side of town and made our way back across town near where we had our first apartment; the nigga linked up with yet another friend of his from way back in the day.

FYI this nigga had a friend in every city. He was just a friendly ass nigga. When you have no job, you have plenty of time to meet random people.

None of them were his actual friends by the way. That nigga didn't give a fuck about anyone, I don't even think he gave a fuck about himself the way he would self-sabotage.

Anyone he called friend was just someone he hadn't fucked over yet. I'd seen him straight fuck over dudes he said were his potna's since day-one.

There was no loyalty in this nigga. How did I expect to get something out of him, that was never in him to begin with? What did I think a motherfucker, that would steal thousands of dollars from his own blood; would take from me?

Steal, Kill and Destroy
Chapter Eleven

Jesus said in John 10:10 King James version that *"the thief cometh not but to steal, kill and destroy."* That was this nigga's agenda from the moment he set eyes on me. You can't convince me otherwise. That nigga never had any intentions to be anything other than the monster that he was.

Let me tell you how this thief stole from me, tried to kill me and destroy my life. Like I was saying, we moved across town and this nigga linked up with a friend of his. This so-called friend was living with his wife, their children, his sister and her roommate at the time. You couldn't keep this nigga from running over there to spend all fucking night there.

This nigga wasn't there all night for his friend. Although he would never admit it, I knew he was trying to get in where he fit in with the roommate, maybe even the nigga sister or both honey I don't fucking know.

He was dedicated to being a bitch nigga. Anything that was legit or made any sense the nigga wanted nothing to do with it. He was always lying and weaseling his way around.

If this nigga put as much energy into obtaining a legitimate living as he did in chasing hoes and pipe dreams, he would've actually made something great out of himself. He had the potential and the drive; he just didn't have the fucking will power to put the shit to good use.

I found out just how much of a lying, trifling motherfucker he was, when I was at my friend's aunt house one night, scrolling through Instagram and I saw him and the roommate bitch damn near hugged up in a picture together. I immediately called the nigga to see what the fuck was going on.

Like the true master of deception that he was, he tried to spin the shit like everyone was just taking pictures. That he had nothing to do with the girl, that she had a boyfriend.

If you wondering if I left, you know good and fucking well bitch that I didn't, so stop fucking playing with me. Yes, for some reason; I still loved this clown of a fucking man. Why I don't fucking know. It's giving crazy right now. Now that I think of it, I must've been.

Call it crazy, call it delusional, call it desperation, call it whatever the fuck you want to call it, you going to do that shit anyway. But what you're not going to do, is call it denial; because I was *never* in denial. I knew good and fucking well he was lying.

I didn't have concrete evidence but the shit was obvious. If we were in a criminal trial, there would've been enough circumstantial evidence to convict this nigga and put him away for life. That's what I should've done, put that nigga away from my life, but we both know I didn't do that or else we wouldn't be here.

That motherfucker played a lot of games with me, and the hardest part to comprehend was that I let him. I did it all in the name of compromise to protect this imaginary peace we never had. Peace we would *never* have. The more I gave the more he took, the more I compromised the more he pushed.

The nigga constantly lied to me, then would accuse me of having trust issues. He cheated repeatedly, then would tell me that I was insecure. This motherfucker stressed me out on a daily, then would tell me I drank too much. He stole every ounce of joy I had then had the audacity to tell me I was boring.

Damn friend. I know I can't be the only one that has ever put up with this type of fuckery. I know there has to be plenty of ex horror stories out there. This one just happens to take the cake.

Here your ass go: *I ain't never been through no shit like this with a nigga.* Good bitch! I don't wish it on you either. But for those of us who have had these types of life experiences, we never thought we would. It's therapeutic to get the shit out. So, if you ain't got shit constructive to add to the conversation then hoe just listen

After a year almost to the day that we lost my first apartment. We were approved for another one. By we, I mean me. We were ecstatic for a new start. Can you imagine living from hotel to hotel for almost a year then finally getting a stable place to live? A new apartment meant possibly a new beginning. I for one was all for it. He seemed happy, maybe this time he was going to finally be the man he claimed to be.

Before we left the hotel, a few weeks before moving into our apartment there was one last stumbling stone that had me contemplating going to my new apartment alone, starting fresh on my own and leaving that nigga behind.

One night he and one of his guy friends went out before I got off work. When I got to the room, I was locked out. I called him and he said that he'd forgotten to drop the key off at my job which was walking distance from the room we were staying in at the time. When I say walking distance, I mean a literal five-to-seven-minute walk.

After speaking to him briefly he said he wouldn't be out long and that he would be back soon to open the door for me. So, I drove to my friend's aunt's house who didn't stay far from the hotel, and sat there for a few hours with my friend; but it was getting late and I had been at work all day. I was tired and just ready to get into the room, take a shower and lie down because I had to be up and back to work the following morning.

I ended up leaving my friend's aunt house who Insisted I stay until I could get back into the room. However, I was mad that I was locked out and upset at his lack of courtesy or urgency to get back to let me in. The last time he talked to me, I was at my friend's house, so he had no idea that I'd left and headed back to the hotel room.

When I got there the nigga still wasn't at the room and what's worse, is that he stopped picking up that cheap ass prepaid phone of his. So, there I was, sitting outside in the parking lot of the hotel, in the dark, in my car; just waiting for the nigga's friend to pull up and drop his ass back off so I could get in the room, shower and get some sleep.

It's been several years since the incident so I don't know exactly what time it was when he pulled up, all I can tell you is that it was late, very late and his friend was nowhere in sight when the nigga pulled up. The same friend who'd picked him up didn't drop his ass off.

Instead, the nigga pulled up with a bitch. It was so dark you couldn't see my car parked in the shadows. I didn't plan the shit, it just worked out in my favor. I also didn't plan for the hoe to park right behind my car either. It was just the luck of the fucking draw I guess.

They could've parked anywhere, but the bitch sealed their fates when she parked behind me. The motherfucker didn't even notice. Both of them got out of the car and he went to the trunk to grab whatever he had in the trunk, but before he walked off, they hugged.

Now, at first, I didn't know it was his ass that pulled up because I'd been out there waiting all night and had seen plenty of cars coming and going, picking up and dropping of guests. He wasn't in the same car he left in, I knew what his friend's truck looked like so, I was completely caught off guard when they pulled up. Not to mention the fact that I didn't expect to see that nigga with a bitch.

So, when they first got out the car and I noticed it was him, my intentions where to sit there like the private detective I was and collect all the evidence so that I could use it against him later. I was ready to catch him in a lie. I wasn't going to say anything this time, I wanted to see how far the nigga would go.

However, things didn't go according to plan after I saw them start to hug. I jumped out of my car in the pitch-black darkness mind you and ran straight for the girl. Not his ass, the girl. Why the fuck did I do that?

I'm smarter than that remember? I'm the pretty, sophisticated intellectual beauty. Well, here was my pretty, sophisticated, intellectual self;

charging out of the shadows in the parking lot of a hotel, like some mad woman, to attack some girl who didn't even know who the fuck I was.

No doubt, lied to and tricked by the same fucking man as me. I'm lucky the bitch didn't pull out a gun and shoot my crazy in love ass over this nothing ass nigga. You know that shit happens right?

However, she never had the chance to reach for anything because before they could release themselves from their little embrace. I had already snatched sister girl up and was beating the fuck out of her.

Now, I'm not just saying this because it's my book. If I would've grabbed her and old girl would've been an ex-marine or some shit and turned around and whipped my ass, I would've put that in here too. I'm going to tell the truth regardless.

It just didn't happen like that. When I launched my attack from the shadows of the parking lot, his ass was surprised too. He didn't know what was going on or who I was at the time. He'd done so much dirt to so many people he thought karma had finally caught up to his ass and someone was pulling his card.

When he realized it was me and that I was beating the fuck out the girl who was dropping him off; he pulled me off the girl.

After I dragged the poor girl, she went to trying to explain that there was nothing going on. That she had only given him a ride. I didn't believe him or her ass because what the fuck ya'll hugging for, if all you were doing was giving him a ride home? Bitch, I don't get out of the Uber and hug my driver, the fuck.

Then he tried me with some shit like it was his friend's sister. I didn't believe that shit either, all I could see was red. So finally, I started beating the fuck out of his ass. When old girl saw that she jumped in her car and pulled off on him.

Now, normally I'm not like that. What got into me, I don't know. Maybe I was just tired of this nigga's bullshit. I'm not defending my actions or anything; I was hella wrong.

All I remember is that after I left my friend's aunt house, I sat in my car a few more hours waiting on the nigga. The more I waited in the car in the cold, the madder I got. I could've stayed at my friend's aunt house. I was more than welcome to; but I felt some type of way about this nigga's total lack of respect and disregard for the fact that I'd worked all day and he didn't even have the decency, to come back to the room on time, to let me in.

Then when he pulls up, he's in the company of a bitch. I just saw red and the rest is history, apparently.

Did he manage to weasel his way out of that situation, barely. He turned the shit around on me saying that I lost control for no reason and that the girl was just someone giving him a ride.

Another mystery that to this day, he has never admitted the truth to. I'm always going to go with my gut though, that nigga was up to no good. I don't care what he says or she said.

Regardless, the nigga manages to make it with me over to the new apartment. I don't know what made me think things would magically become better when we moved.

It was a new start, a new beginning; but it would be the same old nigga and his same old bullshit. This time though, it would be much, much worse. If I thought the devil had any intentions of doing right this time, I was in for a rude awakening. The new place didn't mean shit when it was the same old devil.

By now he didn't even bother to wear a disguise. He walked around in his true form like the monster he was. I remember the first time I found out the nigga was cheating. Not that all the bullshit before wasn't any indication. This time I had irrefutable proof. Nothing this nigga could say to lie his way out of this one. He was caught red-handed.

The hoe made a social media post with a gift I'd given him in the post. The bitch obviously wanted me to see the shit but by this time I was over it and over his ass too. I was dealing with a lot at the time.

My brother's illness had taken a turn for the worst. I had his children with me at the time, all four of them mind you. I was still very young in my twenties; I was working full-time. My plate was full. I didn't have time for this nigga or his bullshit. So, I said fuck it.

My brother whom I'd had a very close, loving relationship with; was in and out of the hospital. He'd come to my apartment a few times; I was trying to make sure he was ok and hoping his health would improve.

I was trying to care for him and his children while this jobless nigga was running around cheating on me. My heart was being ripped both ways as I mourned for my dying brother and my dying relationship simultaneously.

The nigga knew what I was going through and he didn't give a fuck. He knew that my brother was leaving this earth, the exact same way that our father had and it was reopening a painful child hood trauma for me.

I'd confided in him about my childhood, just as he had confided in me about his. I was there for him, whenever he needed me, in every aspect of the way, however he needed me to be. Yet, when I needed this nigga the most, he was in another hoe's bed.

No, not another woman's bed; a literal hoe. I said what the fuck I said. I tell you I can't think of a more worthless piece of shit than this nigga. All this I'm dealing with at one time and here comes this bitch wanting to play on my phone about a nothing ass nigga. Bitch you can have his ass then. The fuck am I holding on to anyway?

I was under a tremendous amount of stress and this nigga couldn't give less of a fuck. When I finally said fuck it, that I was done. The nigga didn't want to leave. Been there, done that shit before. When I pulled away, he wanted to straighten up and do right.

All the dirt this nigga had been doing was coming to light. The bitch knew where my apartment was, she even showed up one Sunday while I was on my way to church. This was right after he decided he didn't want to leave and that he was going to straighten up and do what he could to work things out with me.

Fatal mistake number four. Once a cheater, always a fucking cheater.

I guess the hoe was mad because he cut her off for exposing their little affair to me. So, she shows up to my apartment with her children in the car. I could've lost it; I should have on her ass but I kept my cool that day.

The shit could've really went left but I'm glad it didn't because he just wasn't worth none of that shit. I'm beginning to think it was a mental illness. I should've gone and got the shit checked, because if I'd known then what I know now.

I would've left that nigga at the liquor store.

My brother ended up passing away around that time and though the painful battle with his health was over; it did nothing to ease the emptiness I felt for him leaving me behind in this world and so soon at that.

At the time, I really just needed some support. I didn't want to feel like I was losing everything and everyone all at once. The devil was all I had, so I let him come back around.

He came and held me while I cried and went through my stages of grief. Overwhelming sadness can show you just how alone in the world you are. I swear that was the only thing that saved that nigga back then. That along with the fact that my pussy had started talking to me.

☐ Try ignoring that bitch in the middle of the fucking night when she wakes up screaming feed her dick, see how far that shit gets you.☐ I couldn't blame her though hell, she was starving. She was used to eating 2, 3 and even 5 times a day. To go from having food at your disposal to total restriction can be devastating for anybody.☐

I mean it's not like I didn't try alternatives to change her diet, to wean her away from the nigga. I tried the impossible dick but that shit didn't fool her, she'd spit that shit right out and if by chance I was able to get her to keep it down she would be right back hungry again afterwards.

The shit just wasn't filling or satisfying enough. I had to face the fact that she was a meat eater baby; pure and simple. No genetically modified dicks for her.☐ I am however wiser now; I learned not to listen to the bitch anymore; she talks way too fucking much for her own good anyway and she always gets me in trouble when I do. Her continual weakness would be this nigga's way back in every time. Her need to be held, stroked and comforted for a night or two was all it took, before I knew it, he was back in all the way.

It wouldn't be long either though before that nigga would be back on his bullshit. The next time however, it would be an old hoe. Damn near twice our age. He'd gotten out of his snow bunny stage and was now in his geriatric one.

I couldn't believe I let that nigga deceive me into thinking, that we could actually get pass all the bullshit that we'd been through. That he was done lying and cheating. That's what he was, a liar and a cheater; there's no changing that shit.

I met an old couple once and the man was just flirtatious and inappropriate all the time with the opposite sex. The older woman, his woman, would sit there with a stupid look on her face, while he behaved like a jackass. No doubt, having endured the shit for years and by now, was just used to it. It later came out in an explosive way, that he was cheating on the woman, go figure and the other old bitch pulled up to their house and she got to fighting with her. Shit sounded all too fucking familiar.

All parties were seniors mind you and I thought to myself. Isn't there a point when you grow out of the bullshit? I used to believe that men mature as they age, but this man was a prime example that there were still old fools out there.

I remember thinking, is this what I will have to look forward to, if I continued with this nigga?

The day I found out about this old hoe the devil was fucking with, I couldn't believe I'd let the nigga get me again. Do you remember the butler Steven's face in Django when they killed Calvin Candy? That was my reaction when I found out this nigga was back up to his old tricks again.

I was like *NO* not my little jack rabbit, not again bitch. Just when I'd gotten used to my one thousand pumps in under a minute. Here this nigga go with this bull shit again. Laugh all you want to hoe, at the time I loved his ass and it was all I had. When that's the only dick you've been getting for the last ten years; you look forward to it. He was in and out, like the nigga was robbing a bank; but it was the best thirty seconds of my life.

When I found out he was dicking down seniors, no matter how brief the encounter was; I was beyond pissed. Beyond devastated now because I'd taken him back, forgave him and I couldn't believe that this whack head giving, no dick laying ass nigga, would have the audacity to offer that shit to yet another bitch; while here I am trying to make sense of why anybody would go out of their way to get fucked by the flash.

I can honestly say out of the entire relationship, I've only achieved an organic orgasm with his ass an accumulative total of three times. One I remember quite well because to this day I don't even know *how*, this nigga was able to pull it off. Hell I don't even think he knows either.

I remember it was during make up sex and he was trying to get back in the house and Un regrettably my horny, lonely, desperate ass let him fuck. I don't know where he got the strength to make that shit happen but I'll never forget that day, it's etched in my memory.

It had to be some sort of demonic trickery though because after that he was never able to achieve that shit again. This nigga had to call on the dark underworld to harness that type of demonic dick energy, but you can only keep it for so long. It's too much power for a mortal man to continually possess.

They should've told him that in hell, hell; I wish they would've told me that shit. Here I was thinking I was getting a changed man. New attitude, new perspective, new goals and new dick but none of it was true and none of it lasted. Just deceptive trickery to weasel his way back in.

You can sit there all judgmental and act like I'm the only bitch that done fell for the okie doke, but I refuse to believe that shit. Unfortunately, it happens all too well, to women and men alike. So don't give me that side eye bitch; like you could never. Because I know damn well that you have.

Unlike that first bitch, this old hoe wouldn't go away so easily. She'd stick around through the years. We'd move into another apartment and eventually a house and this nigga would continue this back-and-forth cycle.

I would be the one to let him though, don't think for a second that I don't place any of the blame on myself because I take full responsibility for my part in it.

I watched the devil kill a lot of things that belonged to me. My confidence and self-esteem being high on that list but most bereaved of them all was my dignity.

As much as it would please me, to lay all the blame at his feet. I can't. It's true, he was the mastermind behind the assassination of my dignity; but I was more than a willing accomplice.

He may have pulled the trigger, but I hid the body. I was the one that tried to get rid of all the evidence. I kept all that shit he put me through bottled up because I didn't want anyone to know. I didn't want anyone to see him for the devil he truly was. Why? To project this image of a perfect relationship that didn't exist.

All for what; to save face? I lost a lot of friends and fell out of touch with a lot of family members, because I didn't want to have anything to do with anyone that spoke ill of him. So that meant I had to basically avoid or altogether; cut loose everyone I was familiar with.

I couldn't think of anyone who ever had anything good to say about this man, not one person. That should've told me something right there. Keep in mind I knew his entire family.

The looks I would get; those are the hardest things to remember. Me sitting there trying to pretend as if everything is ok, when the look in everyone's eyes says differently. Now I know what that old lady with the old fool must've felt like.

Who was I fooling other than myself? They knew, they all knew; even Ray Charles could see through that nigga's bullshit.

The very first time I was introduced to a member of his family; the first question she asked me with genuine curiosity in her voice; was what did I see in him?

Bitch if that wasn't a red flag, I don't know what the fuck was. His own fucking family saw no potential, so why the fuck did I? I guess I saw what the fuck I wanted to see.

The motherfucker had stolen years from my life with his buffoonery. I watched him destroy every ounce of hope I had, maliciously and repetitively. I mean what else was left for the motherfucker to do but kill me.

The Devil made me do it
Chapter Twelve

We both know that didn't happen
friend, else I wouldn't be here telling
my story. You were scared for a minute
huh? Thought you lost your new best
friend, didn't you? Yes, you did. I can
tell how you were panic reading. Don't
worry I'm here friend, I aint going
nowhere.

Unfortunately, so many victims of
domestic abuse, be it physical, mental or
emotional abuse aren't' as fortunate as I
am to have escaped their tormentor
with a sense of humor and a positive
outlook on life. Hell, some weren't even
able to escape with their lives at all.

Even though there were many,
many times when I was so stressed from

the shit I was going through with life in general and on top of it being in love with the devil; that I wanted to give up on everything and everyone; myself included. But I never did.

Which is not the flex you think it is by the way. Some things I should've given up on. Some people I should've let go, starting with his ass. When asked, why did I still love him, after all he'd done? why did I stay in the relationship all that time? I could only think of one reason.

"The devil made me do it."

I know it's a phrase made popular by comedian Flip Wilson.

But in all sincerity, I can honestly say he did. He was the reason I fought that girl; he coerced me into taking him back countless times, after numerous offenses. He made me hostile towards anyone that came against him. He deceived me into believing that he loved me and that it was me and him against the world.

So, after the year had ended and our lease was up, we moved to yet, another apartment. We were again in desperate need of a new start. Away from everything and everyone else.

Granted, it was mostly his fault we were starting over again. Bitches had shown up to the apartment while I was there. That was the first indication that I needed a new environment. Remember the hoe who popped up with her kids in the car.

I still don't understand to this day why she would put her children in harm's way like that. I guess she didn't have anyone to watch them. Honestly, and if memory serves me correctly; I believe this nigga was babysitting the hoe's kids.

Just an old sucker ass nigga for a random hoe. Babysitting other nigga's children. No, they weren't his, he was just a sucker nigga doing sucker shit.

Motherfucker's who aren't burdened by employment have time to do that type of simp shit.

The other hoe to show up to my apartment was the old hoe. Now this bitch keyed my charger and flattened the tires on the car, all because this nigga drove it like it belonged to him. I had only two cars at that time and of course he chose to drive my RT Charger.

The amount of time I wasted with this nothing ass nigga on this nothing ass hoe is too much to even fathom, hell; anytime wasted talking about them is too much to spend. So, I'm going to move on for now. I have to pace this shit out. The shit that went on in that situation alone, is a book in itself.

So, needless to say another fresh start was needed when you took into consideration the circumstances.

We found a new love nest, but by now, there was no love to bring to it, only drama and chaos. The trust was completely broken, dreams all shattered. The atmosphere in our home was more toxic than Chernobyl in the spring of 86'. Yet, for some reason though, I was still holding on and I have no reasonable explanation for that type of insanity except to say:

"The devil made me do it."

That is the *only* possible explanation I have and even that shit ain't sufficient enough.

To keep my mind off of the trauma I was dealing with at home, I started working more, a lot more. By this time, I was convinced this nigga was going to do what the fuck he was going to do regardless of how good of a woman I was to him.

Regardless of if I kept a good, clean home. Regardless of if I cooked him delicious home cooked meals. Did his laundry, fucked him whenever he asked me to, catered to his ass, waited on him hand and foot. He was the true definition of a nigga going to be a nigga regardless and ain't shit you can do to change his ass.

He didn't want a good, wholesome, decent woman; because there was nothing good, wholesome or decent about him. I can't say that I ever gave up trying back then, what I will say though is that I didn't care as much as I did in the beginning.

It was around this time I found a work friend that was going through some of the same struggles I was going through. Now, if you ask this hoe; she would try and convince you otherwise.

She's one of them bitches that always act like she could never be in your shoes. Like her situation isn't and would never be similar to yours or as bad as yours; when in actuality, the shit is much worse.

You know the type; kind of like you, bitch.

Anyway, in the beginning me and this hoe was cool, we didn't have any problems we got along quite well. We both worked a lot and we both enjoyed each other's company. I'm going to stop at that for now, we going to circle back around to this hoe later.

So, I was spending all of my free time at work, with my new work friend; which was a good way to earn extra money and also avoid being home at the same time.

I was looking for anything to keep my mind occupied so I didn't have to face life at home with the devil. However, after work, I would still have to come home and deal with whatever bullshit he had there waiting for me.

I learned from the last apartment that a new place didn't necessarily mean a new beginning. With the same nigga, would come the same bullshit. There was nothing wrong with the other apartment, the problem was with the occupants.

Moving didn't mean shit, just a different environment for him to do the same shit in. He would threaten me with his gun at least two more times in this place like he did the last. At least once pointing it in my face at point blank range, telling me that he would shoot me.

This shit would always piss me off because I'd told this nigga about grabbing his fucking gun whenever he was mad at me. Can you imagine telling the man that you love not to point a gun in your face.

It is as insane as it sounds. Plus, not to mention the fact that he never did that shit with another nigga. I've seen a nigga call and threaten his life for fucking the nigga's money over.

It was really the nigga's family member's money but to get to the point. The Devil didn't run over there and draw down on that nigga. He ran over there alright, but it was to pay the man every cent he owed him.

I remember quite well, because he used my car to do it and he didn't waste any time leaving.

That wasn't the first time I watched him flee with fear in his eyes. Another time was when his friend was killed. It could've been him too, he was hanging in this dangerous high traffic drug area that I'd warned him over and over to stay away from.

After everything had gone down and he narrowly escaped with his life; he ran straight home to be held and comforted by me. The same one that if he would've just listened to me, he would've never been in the predicament in the first place.

Regardless, I held and comforted him after the loss of his friend, like he did for me when I lost my brother. Even though I had strong reason to believe that he was again cheating around this time. I put my feelings aside to ease the trauma he experienced, from having someone threaten to take away his life through gun violence. Ironically, like he had done to my life countless times at his leisure.

I already know what you're going to say but damn, I had a heart shit. You're going to make me feel bad for having a heart now? In the beginning you were acting like I was being too rough on the nigga, now you got a problem when I cut him some slack.

Make up your fucking mind. I see you're one of them ole swish swoshy ass bitches; and no hoe, I don't want to hear what you would've done. We're not talking about you; we're talking about me. You and I are two different people; clearly. Damn Ice Queen. Fucking Medusa black hearted ass bitch.

As the years progressed, he resorted to grabbing any weapon he could manage to get his hands on to threaten me with. I figured it would only be a matter of time before he actually used one.

After a year at that apartment and me working hard we would move into a new house. It was supposed to be a new start for us.

But as you may know by now; the devil had another plan.

He was still fucking with his old hoe and by old hoe; I mean decrepit. The new house wasn't too far from the old bitch's senior high rise apartment homes. (Naw, they were regular apartments, the shit just made me laugh to call them that though.) It still doesn't take away from the fact that the bitch was old as shit.

I knew that the old hoe's house was only ten or so miles away but I didn't care, I liked the house and the shit would only be a problem if he entertained the hoe.

Needless to say, the motherfucker did entertain her ass. She'd found out where the new house was too. Till this day he would say he didn't give her the address but you know that nigga's word doesn't mean shit.

The real catalyst behind the move was that I'd gotten promoted at work to store manager and was making a pretty nice salary for the times we were in.

Coincidently this old hoe worked at a fast-food restaurant not too far from the new location I was to manage.

How the bitch found out where I worked? My guess is this loose lip, pillow talking ass, microwave lover told her after giving her that quick dick and having nothing else to offer; he started giving up information about me.

I should've let her old ass have him, he wasn't worth any of the things that I lost. I was earning a good living, doing well. Neither one of them motherfuckers could take it. His ass because I no longer gave a fuck about him and his bullshit and her ass because she wanted to do anything to bring me down to her level or below in hopes that she would finally have any type of advantage over me, because she never could compete or compare.

However, this nigga would be the one to help her try. Talk about sleeping with the enemy. Let me back it up for a moment so you can understand why this nigga teamed up with this hoe in the first place.

Remember I told you earlier that we would discuss how they would get me fired from my job of six years right? Well, that's what we're about to do. They would not only try, but they would succeed too; the only thing in life either of them motherfuckers would ever succeed at; and they couldn't have even done that shit without my cooperation.

Right after I'd just purchased my new vehicle and gotten the new house, this was the low this nigga would stoop to. Knowing that I was taking care of all four of my deceased brothers young children. If I wasn't running behind him like a sad fucking puppy, he didn't know how to exist.

So, I finally let him go, I let him have his old hoe and he realized he didn't want her. She realized in order to keep him she had to aim for me, so she did and he was callous enough to help her. They called the corporate office to my job and told lies about me. With my character in question they couldn't risk their customer's privacy and security. So I was let go and the motherfuckers celebrated that shit.

Two monkeys didn't stop my show. What they didn't count on was my natural God given talent they would awaken in me with their little stunt. What was meant for evil, God turned it around and made it good; but I digress.

Like I said earlier, I was over him, his bull shit and his old bitch. I was ready to let the old hoe have his ass. Something I should've done long before it cost me my fucking job. I guess you live and you learn though.

The next part of this train-wreck of a story takes place during the time when I'd broken up with him and I really mean broken up this time. I had even started seeing someone else.

I can't even begin to tell you the shit storm that came down on me after that. At first the devil seemed ok with the break up. Some space was definitely needed between us.

However, I don't think he intended for me to see anyone. In fact, I'm sure of it. He was the only one allowed to sow his sinful oats. If I wanted some oats, I'd better go make a bowl of Quaker.

What he wanted didn't matter anymore. I was focusing on me and what I wanted; and I couldn't think of anything or anyone I wanted more at the time; then when I saw Dre's fine ass, walk into my job and up to my window to conduct his transaction.

When I tell you all signs were a go. He was handsome, he was fine, the chemistry was there and best of all there wasn't a liquor store around within a five-mile radius.

We exchanged numbers and started talking over the phone to one another. Went on quite a few dates together as well. Restaurants, lounges, movies; you name it, we went. They were just normal dates, but they were a much-needed distraction from the devil and his old lady.

Dre and I would find time to spend together around each other's work schedule. Oh, did I forget to mention that he had a job? Yes, friend, he had a job. He was nice, sweet, kind and respectful. That was the impression I got whenever we went out together. There was nothing wrong with this guy. He was handsome, physically attractive; I mean the whole package.

It was just something in me that didn't let me fully involve myself with him. If you ask me, I'll tell you I don't know what it was. If you asked Dre, he would later say it was because of the Devil.

In the beginning I didn't mention anything about the devil to Dre yet because in my mind I didn't have to, I was single. I could do whatever I chose to do.

Well, all I'm going to say about that; is the devil had another plan.

Dre would find out about him in the most egregious of ways.

The Devil must've felt something in the air, like something was up with me, because the nigga was working overtime to get back in the house.; which for him was the most work he'd done all fucking year. But I wasn't going friend, not at that time.

I'm not going to say I fell for his bullshit again because I don't think that's what it was, that time. What I will say, is that he was just familiar. For some unknown reason I was just drawn back to this man. *I know friend, I see it now, but I couldn't see it back then. I just couldn't. I swore it felt like love at the time.* It didn't matter who tried to come into my life. I already told you I was under his control.

So, he started coming back around like he does whenever he's ready to come back home. After being out in the streets doing God knows what. I didn't let him come back right away for obvious reasons. I had other things going on. I wasn't too worried because I never let Dre know where I lived. A courtesy the devil never extended to me

One day the devil had come over and he and I had gotten into a huge argument. The argument was mainly due to the fact that I was acting, what he called funny. By funny he meant I just wasn't giving him the time of day and I wasn't. I really was tired of his bull shit. Obviously, just not tired enough.

On this particular day. I actually started it out with Dre. We'd had a date that night and was out looking for swim trunks so we could go swimming the following day.
The devil called my phone a bunch of times but I didn't pick up. Finally, he texted me saying he was at my house and that he was busting out all of my windows. So, I ended up leaving Dre before we could even finish shopping for his swim trunks and headed to my house. He was there and of course he hadn't broken any of the windows. He just wanted me to come to the house.

An argument shortly follows and he decided after all this time that he wants his phone back, because the phone I had; he'd purchased for me. So, of course I refused. We get into a tussle over the phone, which he wins. By now, he has his own car; he jumps in his car, and takes off with the phone.

He gets down the street, sees the messages and phone calls between me and Dre and freaks out. I was called every bitch and hoe in the book, *kind of like how I do you friend when you piss me off.*

Now I had a landline in my house, so he calls that and all hell breaks loose. We have a huge argument and I'm telling him we're done we're through. So, he leaves the area. He didn't have to be around the house to know what was going on there.

He still had access to the security system in our house and he would use it to see what I was doing.

That same night I was home alone drinking my wine and relaxing no doubt online shopping for a new phone. It was late and I opened my back door for something, which sent a notification to his phone. At the time, the back door only had a sensor, no camera.

I didn't think nothing of it. I ended up falling asleep. I woke up to him barging in my room and checking the bathrooms and the closet. The nigga had raced to my house in his underwear socks and a housecoat.

He was angry after having went through all my pictures and messages with Dre. I found out later on that he called the poor guy. Keep in mind, he had my cellphone and I didn't know Dre's number by heart.

When I finally talked to Dre, after I got my new phone. He told me that the devil had called him and threatened to shoot up his house. His address was in my text messages as I'd been to his house before.

You can just imagine what went through Dre's head when he saw my number pop up on his screen, only to answer the phone and hear that lunatic on the other line; reciting his address line for line, and issuing threats. But again, I never saw him up the fire on anyone but me.

Dre had no knowledge that the devil even existed. He was heartbroken and devastated as he thought we were going somewhere. When I finally had to have that hard conversation with him it was the shittiest, I ever felt. Somehow in all this, I came out to be the bad person.

"Why didn't you tell me you had a boyfriend?"

"I didn't at the time we met, I mean I still don't. He's just an ex."

"An ex that's acting like this?"

"Yes"

"You know he has my address right?"

"He took my phone, when I went to my house he was there."

"Why did you go back in the first place? You just left me at the hotel, I didn't hear anything else from you then this nigga calls."

"He said he was at my house busting out my windows."

"Then you definitely shouldn't have gone by yourself."

"Can we just talk in person."

"Can you see how I wouldn't trust that?"

"Yeah, I can."

"I thought you and I was good, I'm telling people I have a girl and everything. I'm kissing you and you got a man."

"I don't have a man."

"So, that's why when I asked if you were mine you said no."

"I didn't say no. I just didn't answer you."

"Well, I guess that was my answer then. You're still in love with your ex, that explains so much." he said with a scoff.

"I'm really not though."

"But you really are. That's why we haven't done anything. I was starting to feel like something was wrong with me for a minute; but I know ain't nothing wrong with me."

"There's nothing wrong with you and I'm sorry about all of this."

"Yeah, me too. Look, I have to go do something for my mom."

"Okay".

That was it, he hung up with not even a promise to call me later. I could understand though. He was upset.

He wasn't the only one upset. I thought as I awoke to find the devil standing over my bed, having ridden across town in his underwear to chase someone out of the house that wasn't even there to begin with. He was breathing like a wild, crazed animal, he'd probably did a hundred all the way there.

The same nigga that gave me hoe after hoe problems was standing in my room pissed about a man that didn't even have my heart like he did. I was staring in the face of a half-dressed mad man.

In that moment I couldn't help but flash back to a similar looking mad woman making a mad dash from the shadows of the hotel parking lot to crash out on some unsuspecting girl.

For a split second, I understood his pain all too well because I knew how much it hurts to have to share the one that you love. Then reality kicked in and I remembered the devil doesn't feel pain.

He may have gotten my empathy, if he hadn't run to the kitchen, grabbed a butcher's knife from the drawer and run back into the room. Raise the knife above his head and contemplate stabbing me.

All I remember, is holding up my arms in defense of the sharp blade and repeating over and over that I hadn't done anything with Dre. That much was true.

I never felt so vulnerable or helpless in my life, not even with the gun if that makes any kind of fucking sense at all.

After an intense face off, he finally dropped the knife and retreated. He was out the door and gone just as quickly as he had come. A fucking phantom menace.

I knew what he did wasn't okay. Nowhere in my mind did I think that was a normal way to treat someone you claim to love.

I knew I should seek some type of help, but something had a hold of me and as bad as I wanted to help myself. I didn't want to risk hurting him. As much as he had hurt me, I couldn't see myself causing him any type of pain. I couldn't see myself having the police punish him no matter how much he deserved it.

I was conflicted and I felt emotionally trapped. In my mind this was just another bad day, it would get better, it had to. I can hold out a little longer for better, right? So, I was left alone in my empty room wondering when better would come or if I would ever be free from the stronghold this man had over me.

The amount of regret I feel for not having the strength to leave is immeasurable. I feel like my young self, owes my older self an apology for the hell she put me through; if that makes any sense. The bad memories she created, that I still have to live with to this day. Memories that I try not to think about too often.

I feel like she not only owes me an apology but young Dre as well. But since he isn't here and neither is she. I'll try to do my best.

Even though we're both grown, and more mature; (at least one of us I'm sure). It's never too late to say what needs to be said. What should've been said. I don't feel there's a Statute of limitations on an apology.

So Dre, if you're listening; if you're reading. I'm sure you never in life want to speak to me again, and I can definitely understand why. I just want to say that I now realize, that I never gave you the chance you deserved.

You tried; and I did notice. My mind just wasn't in the right headspace to receive your kindness and affection. I was lost, and I couldn't find myself in time enough to give us the chance to become what we had the potential to be, and for that; I'm deeply apologetic. I wish I could go back in time, but we both know that can't happen. You gave me enough years, and enough chances, to come to my senses. So I won't take up any more of your time, just know that if I could go back in time and pick again, I'd choose you in a heartbeat; but I guess too little, too late. Should've chose you when I had the chance. I know it's a lucky girl out there somewhere.

That's all I'm going to say on that subject. Friend, if you're still reading; give me a minute before we start the next chapter. I'm going to go grab me a glass of wine. I'll meet you on the next page.

A Deal with the Devil
Chapter Thirteen

You can probably surmise by how the last chapter ended, that I had indeed let the devil back in. Why; you ask. What was wrong with Dre? Absolutely nothing; not a got damn thing. The problem wasn't with him at all; it was with me.

Blinded by emotion I was set on loving this man and nothing anyone said or did could deter me. Not even the fact that he didn't love me back.

Of course, he said it with his mouth, he said a lot of shit out of his mouth; but that didn't make it true. His actions showed something completely different.

Yet, I was willing to throw caution to the wind and open my severely wounded heart back up to him again. So, for the umpteenth time; I took him back.

I was already in up to my neck, I figured what else did I have to lose?

Dre hadn't fully given up on us yet, he was the only one fighting for whatever it was that we had. He would spend a couple years fighting that battle.

However, I discontinued my romantic pursuit of him and communication with anyone else for that matter, that posed a threat to our reconciliation. I was focused and committed to making it work. I'd been through so much with this relationship; if there was a light waiting for me at the end of this long dark tunnel than maybe it would've all been worth it.

Yes, bitch, we started over but this time I had his word that things were going to be different. He had this whole plan to get us back on track. It was a verbal contract; an agreement of sorts if you will.

Despite having been let down several times in the past by this man, I was intrigued by his offer and thought no harm could come of hearing out the terms. The conditions were fair, no different than your standard, boilerplate, verbal relationship contract and pretty much just as binding.

There were a few stipulations on fidelity outlined but that was expected given his track record. We'd thought of everything. I was even savvy enough to throw in a clause where we got at least one date night a week to go out and spend time together, you know enjoy each other's company. We were locked in; we were determined to make it this time.

I admit, I was skeptical at first. I questioned whether I had the emotional capacity to enter into this agreement. He assured me however, that he would fulfill all of his contractual obligations.

So, I signed with my heart. I had a new lease on love and all it cost me was my soul. That motherfucker would be back to his old ways before the ink could dry.

Someone should have told me that you never make a deal with the devil. It may look like your dreams are about to come true but, in the end, you always get way more than you bargained for.

Like a crazy white hoe sending me harassing emails and coming to my house to pick his bitch ass up during an argument. I never saw that shit in the contract, maybe I should've read the fine print; because nowhere in it did he mention he would spit on me in my driveway and flatten three tires on my brand new challenger before hopping in the car with the bitch with $600 in cash he'd stolen from my purse.

I thought shit like that only happened in Tyler Perry movies. No, for real. When I was younger, I used to watch his plays and movies and I would always say, no one is that fucking mean Tyler.

Honestly, I would look at the characters and say this is too much, people don't treat people like this. Especially people they claim to love, people that they sleep with.

I was a teenager then, ain't ignorance bliss. Now that I'm older I see that Tyler was on to something. He knew exactly what the fuck he was talking about.

Yet through it all I stayed. Through the continual lying, cheating and broken promises; I stayed. Through the physical, emotional and psychological abuse, I stayed. Why?

No, that was a real question. This isn't part of the book no more bitch; this is a cry for help!

Why the fuck did I let this bum ass nigga do me like that, friend?

It feels just like what Ashanti said in her song Foolish. "All the things that we accept, will be the things that we regret." I'll be damned if she wasn't right.

It'll be women like me: *and I know you bitches are going to say I'm the only one that's been through this type of bullshit but I beg to differ.* that'll be the type of women men say are "damaged" and have "baggage" now.

If that's the case, then like who the fuck caused the damage? I didn't do this shit to myself. I did everything they recommend a "good woman" do and nothing good came out of that shit.

I stood behind him, I motivated him, I encouraged him, I tried to do the right thing for us both and where did that shit get me? I was the ride or die. Next time if it's ride or die then just kill me bitch because I'd rather die than go through that shit again.

I wish I could've seen this at the time; because at the time you couldn't convince me, that wasn't love.

It's not like some didn't try. For the most part, I kept a lot of things hidden. I was too ashamed to admit what I was going through, and that I'd let something like that happen.

To the very select few that I chose to open up to, they didn't feel like much help at all at the time. The first thing bitches like to do is get up on their high horse and act as though they've never been through shit.

If I had to listen, to one more fake ass, independent, boss bitch, Ms. I don't need a man for nothing ass hoe; try to explain my motherfucking worth to me. I was going to lose my motherfucking mind. Bitch, I know my worth. It's him I'm trying to get to see the shit.

These types of bitches would rather shame you then help you. Majority of the ones saying what you'll never catch them doing really should be saying what you'll never catch them doing again. Just faking the funk. Trying to pass off shame and criticism as advice. Sometimes the best advice is none at all, especially if you're going to talk out the side of your neck and then go do the same shit you told me not to. And I swear it be the same bitches going through or that has been through worse.

I kid you not. I have confided in a bitch and she will point out everything I did wrong, he did wrong and will swear she could never and not even a few years, months or even weeks later; the bitch will be in a worse situation with a nigga; and will just be taking the shit.

But see I listen, and I don't judge. One thing I learned is to never say never because you never know when you may be in a similar situation. Now let's see if you apply all that good advice, you were giving me; to your situation.

They don't and they won't. Just like the bitch I was telling you about last chapter. I said we were going to circle back around to that hoe and here we are. I couldn't end this story without putting this hoe on blast.

Now this bitch a so called "friend of mine". You know you have to watch out for the ones that call themselves your friend. This hoe, who had recently just gone through her own bullshit, with the father of her children, not too long before my problems began or should I say came to a head; because my problems had been there since the beginning.

Anyway, over the course of our short friendship, which lasted maybe two or three years give or take, we confided in each other about our relationship problems. That was my first mistake with this bitch. My second one was letting this hoe get comfortable to where she thought she could talk to me any kind of way about my life.

Now I admit, I offered her advice when she was going through her bullshit with her children's father; but I never criticized her the way she always did me and I never called her out her name. Just comfortable child, but don't worry; I nipped that shit in the bud real quick.

That's why we're not cool to this day. It's a wonder why I couldn't do that with his ass. I would've saved myself the headache.

Anyway, this bitch and I'm just going to say her name because bitch you earned it. Kianna was able to break away from the hold her child's father had on her and in my opinion this nigga was just as bad as the devil, if not worse.

The shit he took her through could be a whole other book in itself. I would write it too, but I don't want to team up with that hoe. She showed me her true colors when she met her new nigga.

When we both were going through at the same time, the bitch was humble. But when she found a new man, all that hoe could do was criticize me and mine. This was the same nigga I was with when you were with your no good as baby daddy and you ain't have none of that energy then because you were going through shit in your relationship too. All of a sudden, now that you done switched up on him, I guess you decide to switch up on me too, right? Cool.

Now don't get me wrong, I take criticism well when it's constructive but don't think you're just going to talk to me crazy and if you feel like he did; well, bitch you ain't him.

Wasn't no real love lost anyway because oh, don't think the hoe was ever a true friend. All she did was run my business back to other hoes; (her other friends) because we didn't run in the same circle.

We were work friends that got close, a little too close for comfort. She gave weird vibes too checking my nigga's social media page, just to hold conversations with me about his posts.

I knew her new nigga too, was good friends with him and never sent the nigga a friend request. It was giving obsession with my relationship to the point I had to check her, on multiple occasions; about constantly having something to say. I'm like bitch, you worked through yours, let me work through mines hoe; without your negativity.

It never seemed to come from a genuine place of love. Just some random off the wall offensive shit, that I knew you were holding tea time with your other friends about. I got that vibe when I met the hoes.

Even though she was right about the circumstances she went about it all wrong.

Because I know you're reading. I just want to know what did you gain from being right; since you were so obsessed with it. How much money did you win? Or was the look on my face, when that nigga finally did me in; priceless.

I wasn't trying to do anything but save *my* relationship. I didn't want to end up like you and your children's father. I thought we could fix our shit, before it got that bad. I guess that's what I get for thinking huh?

Well, that's all I'm going to say on that subject. I ain't got no smoke with you, bitch. I'm saving my energy for this nigga. Next chapter hoe, you had your five minutes of fame.

The Devil to Pay
Chapter Fourteen

As a result of my continual devotion to the devil, I paid a hefty price. I was in way over my head. By now Bitch I was drowning and the only person I wanted to save me; was holding my head under the fucking water.

I wish someone would've warned me about bargaining with the devil. I wish someone would of told me before I made the agreement that The Devil never keeps his word.

Hell, I wish someone would've told me that he would declare his love for a renowned, self-proclaimed prostitute before the world like Sergeant Phil Cantone in Harlem Nights. Then skip town with the hoe only to try and come back not even a month later after the shit went south. Yeah, that clause was left out of the agreement.

If I would've gotten the shit in writing, I would've been able to get his ass for breach of covenant. Since I didn't, it just deemed our new lease on love null and void.

He extended another bargain, offering to renegotiate the terms of course. But, given the circumstances; I thought it best if both parties went their separate ways.

However, with the forfeiture of the agreement. He would be required to relinquish ownership of my soul.

A heavy price to pay but the good news in all of this is that I paid the price so that you don't have to. Let this tale be a cautionary warning to you before you decide to have a dalliance with the Devil.

Oh, did I mention that the nigga ran off with the hoe on Valentine's Day of all motherfucking days; if you can believe that shit. Ain't *that* some romantic shit? So, I thought it only fitting that my book be released on the same day. Instead of allowing this motherfucker to ruin the holiday for me forever, I'm going to turn it into the day my book debuts and the day I sell the most copies. Tragedy into motherfucking triumph!

The tug of war on my heart had come to an end and when it was finally over it hurt worse than when I was going through it.

If anyone has had any kind of surgery you know that the recovery is the worst part. During the operation you get anesthesia to numb the pain. That's what I had during the removal of this nigga from my heart. I had small doses of him during the excision to anesthetize the pain.

That's exactly what removing him felt like, open heart surgery. Girl, I had a nigga-ectomy' and I must say it was devastating but absolutely necessary.

There was a tremendous amount of downtime afterwards but this operation wasn't for cosmetic reasons, this was an essential, vital life sustaining procedure. I mean at this point; the nigga was a health risk. He was literally draining the life from me. He was a soul snatcher and I'm not talking about the good kind either.

Although the operation may have been a success. Sometimes I wonder if it was my only option for wellness.

You ever hear of after a break up, you write down all the good shit and all the bad shit and if the bad outweighs the good detrimentally; then you've made the right decision. Well, I tried it and this shit turned into a motherfucking book!

Friend, do you remember that song by Mary J not gon cry. Of course you do, who the fuck do I think I'm talking to? Everybody remembers that song. Well, that's exactly how I felt, I was fed up. Enough was enough. I was not gon cry. That was me, every word of it friend.

Naw, for real I can't even lie; bitch I cried. I cried like a motherfucker. I cried worse than a baby with colic. Shit I cried every day for like a year straight.

I know what you're thinking, I already know what Bri' Trilla said. "We ain't crying over no niggas, we ain't riding by no nigga house spying on no niggas." Yep, that's exactly what was on your fucking mind.

Judgmental ass hoes like you are easy to read. But friend, it wasn't even over him this time. Shit, the tears were for me. I was in shock how I let this nigga play me like that. Key word being let, because I do take responsibility for my part.

I ignored every red flag thinking I could change a nigga, thinking I could save a nigga, that didn't want saving. I thought he was just misunderstood, that he had a lot of demons to fight and I could be the woman to help him fight them. Little did I know that motherfucker was the demon; and soon, I would be the one in need of help. You know what the hardest part of the breakup was?

Nope, not losing him because I realized I wasn't losing shit worth holding on to. The hardest, most difficult part, was giving up and letting go. I'm the type of person that doesn't believe in giving up.

I know that I can do anything I put my mind to and it's hard for me to get to a certain point in something and just say fuck it. It ain't gon work, it ain't gon happen. I believe it'll work, if you work it. I'm ten toes down, I'm all in. I'm gone ride this thing to the wheels fall off.

That's way too much loyalty, devotion and power to give to a person; let alone the devil.

For a long time, I asked myself over and over again, why did this happen to me? What had I done wrong to deserve this type of treatment? Then it dawned on me. That I hadn't done anything wrong. That you don't have to do anything for the devil to set his sights on you. He desired to have you, to sift you like wheat from the beginning.

I used to think, if the nigga didn't love me, if he truly didn't want to be there, then why waste either of our time? Who has ten years to waste like that? Then I realized, he wasn't wasting his time; only mine. The Devil isn't bound by time like we are. I was the only one missing my destiny while he was fulfilling his.

The Devil had my mind so convoluted that when God finally set me free, it didn't feel like a victory at all, it felt like he was punishing me. But friend, what I thought was a soul-crushing blow turned out to not be that at all. Where I thought I'd failed, I'd actually prevailed. You might find it hard to believe from the way that I talk about it but I don't harbor any hatred toward him at all, even though he is the devil. I don't wish any ill will upon him.

In fact, I hope he gets all that he deserves. I hope, everything that he put out into the universe; he gets back 1000-fold and that's from the heart. How's that for well wishing?

But you know what else though friend, every now and again the devil will try and see if he still has any power over me. To see if I'm truly saved, set free and delivered and you know what I tell him friend?

No, I don't backslide friend; that isn't me anymore. I rebuke that devil, tell him get thee behind me Satan. It doesn't stop him from trying though.

Is it tempting?

What do you want, a lie or the truth?

Because I can give you a lie and tell you that I don't wish there was a good ending to our story, and part of me, a tiny part; that still doesn't believe that we could make it, if we really tried.

But the other part of me knows now that there is no "making it" with the devil. He is known as the enemy therefore he cannot be an ally or a companion no matter how hard you work. He is always working against you. Sabotaging any relationship, you try to build with him. He doesn't want peace and love he wants chaos and anarchy and he wants to make you believe that it's you.

He wants to make everyone believe it's you including you because not only does he want to waste your time but he wants to destroy all hope for your future; one that you can have with the right person God intended for you to be with. He wants to rob you of your identity and destroy your reputation as well, so that not only will you not believe in yourself but no one else will either.

If we let him win like that sis, then he has robbed us of our entire purpose. We can't let the devil win.

Does the hurt and pain ever go away? Honestly, that's not a question I can answer right now, but as soon as it does, I'll let you know. What I can say though is that it gets better, it gets a hell of a lot better.

Although I'm aware that I was in an abusive relationship, I don't consider myself a victim of domestic abuse. I wouldn't even go as far as to call myself a survivor of it either.

There are too many men and women to count, most of whom aren't here today to tell their story, who have endured far greater atrocities from monsters that were far worse. than I can imagine.

I would never try and bring myself equal to them. What I will say is that I survived the devil. He tried to take me out but I survived. I'm a living testimony. I made it sis and I know that if I can; anybody that crosses this motherfucker's path can too.

See how I called you sis this time. I ain't cursing you out no more since you've come down off that high horse. You humbled yourself; that's good. Before, you were all judgmental, acting like it couldn't have been you.

Well, bitch I'm glad it wasn't you too. I wouldn't wish that shit on my worst enemy. You can say that I was stupid if you want to. You think I give a fuck about being called stupid? Bitch, I've been called worse. I ain't the first stupid bitch and I won't be the last. You've been stupid before too hoe; you just refuse to admit the shit. See, you making me talk crazy to you again. Just when I thought we had an understanding..

. Anyway, I wrote this book, not to serve me but to serve as a precautionary tale to anyone who see the red flags and choose to still ignore them.

Even if you don't see the red flags, but those characteristic signs of Satan start showing up in that man you're dating or that woman you fall in love with; and yes, fellas do not be deceived.

The devil can show up in many forms. Just remember, I warned you. That he's out there, going to and fro, seeking whom he can devour through false friendships, kinships and relationships.

Take heed and don't say I didn't warn you. Tread lightly, so that you're not deceived; and you aren't the next one to fall In Love with the Devil.

Thank you so much for reading...

I hope you had as much fun reading ILWTD as I had writing it. If you enjoyed this book, then check out my other titles
The Account (Part I) Available for purchase now
The Account (Part II) Available for purchase now
The Account II The kingdom vs Autumn (Part I) Coming Soon
The Account II The Kingdom vs Autumn (Part II) Coming Soon

In everything that we do, read, study or watch I feel that's it's important to get something out of it. This book was written for entertainment yes, but it was also created for reflective and thought-provoking purposes as well. Proverbs 4:7 says Wisdom is the principal thing; therefore, get wisdom, and with all thy getting get understanding. So, the next part of the book is called what did we learn? The last three numbers were left blank for you to fill in on your own with what you actually took away from the experience.

What did we learn?

1. If you meet a nigga with nothing, leave his ass with nothing. Or just leave altogether your choice, but the old woman was 1000 percent right on this one. She had to have been some sort of philosophical genius or something; certainly ahead of her time because that type of wisdom and enlightenment don't grow on trees.

2. Men are not DIY projects. This isn't build a bear ladies. Men are supposed to come already assembled. The only thing you're going to create is a fucking monster if you try to build on top of bull shit. Good men come ready made by mothers, fathers, grandparents and so on.

3. Class ended after high school, whatever you didn't learn from your teachers, your mother or your father; I don't have the time, energy, patience or the credentials to teach you now.

4. Number four can easily be placed at number one as well, but never and I mean never; let a fuck nigga get away with fuck shit. He get away with that shit once, he going to do that shit again. Hold his ass accountable for whatever bullshit he does. If he looking for three strikes tell his ass to go play baseball.

5. Let her have his bitch ass, because there shouldn't be a *her* in the fucking first place. Give him to her, she ain't winning shit, I guarantee you. Could've saved myself a lot of fucking time and trouble had I let the first hoe take the nigga off my hands.

6. Do not bypass the warning signs. They are there for a reason. They are letting you know that hazardous conditions are ahead if you continue down that road.

7. Never make a deal with the devil. Whatever promises he makes you, he never intends to keep, he only intends to keep you around with them. If you stay, there will be hell to pay.

8._____
_____
_____
_____

9._____
_____
_____
_____

10._____
_____
_____

Made in the USA
Columbia, SC
09 February 2025

53067246R00133